RUTHLESS SENTINEL

VICIOUS VIPERS MC 2

LYNN BURKE

RUTHLESS SENTINEL

Working security for my MC brother, I'm tasked with protecting a crooked judge who targets his willful daughter with emotional abuse.

She's beautiful. She's confident and has a backbone of steel, but I recognize the pain in her eyes.

She distracts me from my job, and echoes of Pop's taunts of my being a failure fester in my head.

But I will prove him wrong.

I will withstand our connection, the relentless pull between us.

I will protect her family—*her*—from the unknown enemy, even if it costs me my soul.

DEDICATION

For Avril

CONTENTS

STONE

L ess than two hours in Judge Burtonelli's presence, and I wanted to flatten his goddamn nose. Kick his ass rather than protect it like I'd been hired to do. I'd been put in charge of his personal security detail after a few death threats scared the shit out of him. What did he expect running for the Senate with a hard stance on cleaning up Massachusetts's drug problems would get him? Roses and champagne?

Maybe from his rich-ass supporters who'd planned a party for the night with over three hundred invites sent out and RSVP'd. I held the guest list in hand, scanning quickly for names I might recognize. A handful from the news and another dozen or so Hollywood types planned to attend the Christmas Eve party.

Not *my* people, that was for damned sure.

Salt of the earth, my bastard of a father had called us. Hard working blue collars who ran the damn country, military grunts and brats. Hard asses who didn't know what a cushy life felt like. My kind of people.

"Where the hell is she?" Burtonelli barked as we waited in their mansion's foyer, and I glanced up from the elite list of individuals sure to donate millions to his campaign fund.

His wife fussed with his tux tie, making shush noises, the overhead chandelier glinting off the sequins in her silver gown's bodice. "She's on her way."

"Late. As always." Burtonelli's tone revealed his scowl as I glanced at their other two children, Marisa and Cristian. While the older daughter looked just like their dark Italian father and had followed in his footsteps to become a lawyer, the younger boy looked fresh out of high school and took after their blonde mother. Both, thank fuck, seemed to have inherited her meeker spirit, too.

My Viper brother and fellow Tellier Security

employee, Greed, stood beneath the circular stairs beyond the family in a black on black suit, fiddling with his ear piece. He raised a brow when I met his gaze.

Lips pursed, I shoved the list into my suit coat's inner pocket and glanced at my watch.

Their middle child, Giada, was supposed to have shown up at her parent's home twenty minutes earlier, since the family was to ride together to the night's event.

"She's doing this on purpose." Burtonelli pushed away his wife's motherly handling and straightened his wool overcoat. "Selfish from day one, that child. Why can't she be more like her sister and put family above her own wants?" His glance at Marisa lightened his pissed off expression, and I found my stomach clenching.

A muscle in my jaw ticked. I'd never met their other daughter, but I'd learned a lot about her in the previous forty-eight hours since Warden had taken on the pain in the ass job and put me in charge. Giada was the wild child, the black sheep. The Burtonelli who went her own way rather than go into law like her sister, father, and his father before him. A model who had begun to make a name for herself. And from pictures I'd seen, she was gorgeous as fuck with black hair and bright green eyes—a mix of both parents.

Had she gone her own way out of rebellion? To pay her father back for his obvious lack of love for her? His calling her selfish hadn't been the first negative thing about her I'd heard out of his mouth since meeting him—and I doubted it would be the last.

I couldn't handle bullying. Hearing and seeing that shit sent me down a dark path of memories I'd spent most of my life trying to rise from. Ashes of the past, drying to the soul.

For your own good, Pop had told me dozens of times. He'd taught me how to be a hard bastard, not easily provoked—unless I saw another person experiencing similar treatment I'd known as a kid. That kind of shit threatened my self-control like nothing else.

"She's here," a deep voice said in my ear piece, bringing my focus back on my job—where it should have been.

"Your driver said Giada has arrived," I told the Burtonelli family, tugging on my own coat.

"We should have just left her behind."

I fought to keep from glaring at Burtonelli, who'd insisted countless times the family needed to arrive together, bonded and strong behind him since—according to TV ads—he valued family above all else.

Lying fuck, same as everyone with political ambitions.

His wife's smile wobbled, and she struggled to put her own coat on.

Cristian stepped forward to help her as his father stalked toward the front door.

"I'll let her in," I told him, stepping in his way, more to protect a woman I hadn't yet met than to act according to my job as his guardian.

A blast of cold air hit my face, but my breath caught for an entirely different reason as subtle lilac and vanilla scents swirled around me.

Giada Burtonelli stood on the granite stoop, coat gaping open to reveal a jade-colored dress that wrapped around her body, cradling the type of tits I wanted to fuck. Tiny, tucked waist, perfect for the span of my hands. The skirt's center split to display the top of her thighs, inches from the apex of where I bet heaven lay in wait—much too fucking short. Toned legs, tanned and smooth, led to spiked heels porn stars wore while getting their asses fucked.

My dick jolted, and I clenched my jaw against the combustion of lust that roared to life in my balls.

Lifting my focus off her hot as fuck body to her face didn't help matters. Eyes, green as spring grass, sharp as a damn Samurai sword, pierced through me with the type of instantaneous connection that robbed a man of his identity. Her full lips parted on a quick intake of air as her focus moved upward over my body to meet my gaze.

I'd seen pictures. Knew she'd be beautiful, but I didn't expect my breath to be ripped from my lungs or the hairs on my body to stand at attention because of the energy crackling between us.

"You're late!" Burtonelli barked from behind me.

Giada's eyes hardened as she lifted her pointed chin, her ruby red lips thinning into a line.

I moved back, fucking tongue-tied.

"Hello to you, too, Father." Low and husky, her voice thickened my dick even more.

"Could you make an effort to be on time just once, Giada?" Burtonelli moved toward her, his scowl raking down over her. "What the hell are you wearing?"

"Oscar," she snipped her reply, her eyes flashing.

"You look like a whore. Fitting, I suppose, since you can't seem to keep your legs closed to every Tom, Dick, and Harry who shows interest in you."

I blinked, but her façade didn't crack. Not the

first time she'd heard such a thing, I expected as my fists clenched, but not my monkey...

Her father stalked past her. "I specifically said to *be on time*," he continued. "You know how important this night is." Stomping down the granite stairs toward the waiting limo in the circular drive, he muttered about people contributing to his campaign and what they might think of his daughter's inappropriate attire—and the fact it was too late for her to change.

"You look lovely, dear," Giada's mother said, stepping forward, hands outstretched.

Kiss, kiss—fake as hell, before Mrs. Burtonelli hurried after her husband as though he tugged her along with a leash.

Marisa came next to greet her sister, her face pained as though empathetic toward Giada being her father's verbal punching bag, but it was Cristian's infectious grin and grabby hands to hug her that brought a smile to Giada's face.

And Christ, what a smile. Dimple, flashing white teeth, eyes alight with enough joy to slam an uppercut into my gut, stealing my breath again.

I stared as they hugged, jealousy slithering in like a damn snake to wrap coils around my stomach and squeeze. Possessiveness wasn't something I'd felt before, but fuck if I didn't recognize its gut-twisting presence—even if it was her brother putting his hands on her.

Stretching my neck side to side, I tore my attention off the two siblings whispering to one another and glanced at Greed who watched me with a smirk on his face.

I scowled and spun to follow Marisa outside. I should have been the first into the night even though Burtonelli's personal guards already awaited us in the circular drive out front, but everything about Giada distracted me.

My scowl deepened. *Focus.*

The plan had been for Greed to ride in the limo with the family while I took shotgun in the lead car, but I decided on a change while scanning their gated property in the darkening sky.

Three Burtonelli guards, including their driver and head of security who'd been placed beneath my command for the duration of the contract, stayed positioned where I'd commanded along the drive. All of us were connected by top of the line earpieces provided by Tellier Security.

The driver stood by the car's back door as Mrs. Burtonelli slid inside, the other two packing with heads swiveling where they waited by the cars boxing the limo in.

Hairs on my neck stirred, but without any sense of impending danger.

Giada.

I could feel her focus on my back like a soft caress, a whisper of fingertips along my spine, but I didn't turn, even after the mansion's front door slammed shut.

Fighting off shivers and my body's distraction from my job, I strode toward the limo, waving the driver away. Cristian moved into my periphery as I pulled up by the opened door, and he slid in behind his oldest sister.

I feigned disinterest as Giada neared in a cloud of sweet, subtle lilac laced with vanilla.

My hand moved on its own, offering her assistance even though I continued to scan the property, senses beyond alert, my body strung fucking tight as hell.

Her smooth fingers danced across mine, and I gripped tight in sudden need to yank her close. Soothe the hurt her father had inflicted that she'd tried to hide behind a mask of who-gives-a-shit stubbornness.

I turned my focus on her face—she stared up at

me, her eyes wide and lips parted. Currents raced through our clasped fingers, straight to my dick.

"Giada!" Her father's annoyed call from inside the limo jerked her attention off me, and I grit my teeth while she bent down to get into the limo and join her family.

I released my hold on her hand and fought the need to watch her ass as she climbed into the limo. Greed approached, his inquisitive stare on my face.

"I'm riding with them," I told him, my tone not welcoming argument or question.

"Right-o, boss man," he said with a grin, touching his forehead in a fake salute. He sauntered toward the lead car, and I inhaled a bracing breath before following Giada, the non-princess, into the lion's den.

I told myself I'd made the hasty decision thinking my presence would keep tempers from rising into a barrage of bullying, which I had a feeling Burtonelli had every intention of continuing.

He started in on Giada before the door closed behind me. "Marisa was in court this afternoon and she still managed to arrive on time."

Cold eyes and an even colder smile met his scowl across the distance separating father and daughter. "Good for her."

My lips twitched. At least she didn't take any shit.

"Watch your tone, young lady!"

"Sorry, Father." Her voice didn't sound the least bit contrite.

"What were you doing that was so damn important? Taking off your clothes for another photographer?"

"As a matter of fact, yes."

Lucky bastard, whoever he was.

"And I suppose you fucked him as well."

Giada stared him down, lips sealed as jealousy coiled around my stomach.

Burtonelli muttered something beneath his breath—including the word "whore" again.

Acid burned my gut.

"What a disappointment." Burtonelli huffed and sat back, tossing his hands in the air. "You're not as smart as Marisa or Cristian, Giada, but you could have done something more with the life I've offered. Free college education. A position in my old firm. Instead, you're stripping for strangers to take pictures that you'll never be able to put behind you should you decide to one day get your head out of your ass."

"The last thing I wanted to be was a lawyer," Giada replied, cool as a fucking cucumber. "And for your information, the photographer was a *woman*. Not that you'd care."

"I know why you're doing this," the judge continued as though she hadn't spoken, "and don't think it will work."

Giada raised an eyebrow but kept silent, her hands lightly folded in her lap. To the rest of the world, she might appear unfazed, but I'd learned to see beyond the eyes, reading microexpressions as easily as a kids' bedtime story.

Before her seemingly bored brow raised, a line furrowed between, disappearing before most would have caught it. The twitch downward on the corners of her lips also betrayed her sadness. Her pain.

"Anything to gain the spotlight," her father muttered.

His wife touched his arm in attempts to stop him. "Dear—"

"A fashionably late entrance to get the attention you crave," he all but spit at his younger daughter.

"Perhaps if I'd been given more attention as a child, I wouldn't be so desperate for it now," Giada had the balls to toss out with a bit of bite in her voice.

Fuck, how I wanted to clap.

"Giada," her mother chided softly as the judge's face reddened.

"Perhaps," her father seethed, his brow furrowed, "if you'd showed one *ounce* of respect for your elders, you would have!"

"I've been on my damn best behavior since you announced you wanted to run for the Senate, Father," Giada shot back, her fingers tightening their hold on one another. "Not one misstep. Not one whisper of scandal or inappropriate pictures, and yet you still find something to bitch about."

"How you've managed, is beyond me."

"Nicolo," the judge's wife tried again, but he brushed her off, same as before.

"You're going to end up pregnant out of wedlock because of that group of friends you run around with. Or, in jail for a DUI. Imagine what that will do for this family's image. As if you haven't done enough damage already!"

I'd had about enough—but a voice in my ear let me know we were five minutes out.

I held up a hand as the judge opened his mouth to spew more shit at his silent daughter who fought to keep the effects of his words off her face. "We're five minutes away from the hotel and need to go over the details of our arrival."

Lips pursed, he nodded, and I launched into how I expected the five of them to exit the vehicle and make their way inside the hotel hosting the event. To avoid distraction, I kept my focus off Giada even though her gaze singed me.

Burtonelli had insisted on a front entrance drop off rather than the hotel's underground parking lot which offered more protection. I'd given in to his "need" to be seen on the red carpet, his arrogant insistence on putting his supposed loved ones' lives in danger.

And he called *Giada* selfish. Fucking narcistic prick. She'd be better off leaving the family, same as I'd done with mine. Independence. Freedom to be what one wanted. Freedom to make one's own way in life without negative influence or pressure.

Sure, she'd moved out three years earlier from what I'd learned, but she hadn't yet escaped the Burtonelli name and the shit that came with it.

I'd chosen a life of violence, earning my black belt in karate rather than self-medicate with sex, booze, and drugs, and eventually opened a dojo where I could teach kids and women how to properly protect themselves—with self-confidence rather than fear.

Because of my life's choice, I could protect our

clients from close-up threats, but if someone wanted to take Burtonelli out from a distance, the surrounding buildings in Boston's downtown would offer the perfect lay-in-wait spot for a sharp shooter.

My intuition, alertness, fists, and ability to wield a gun could only offer so much. But I'd been paid to do my best—nothing would keep me from focusing. Not even a gorgeous, young woman whose mere presence acted like a live wire touching my skin, and whose unsettling, true emotions couldn't be hidden. At least, not from me.

Even considering the fucked situation, I could feel her stare. Smell her sweetness. Taste the instantaneous lust sparking between us. Empathize with her inner pain.

I wanted to hold her close. Punch out the judge, or at least give him a piece of my damn mind about the damage words inflicted on tender souls—oftentimes more than fists.

But I couldn't be distracted. Warden trusted me. I needed to stay out of the family drama and focus on what needed to be done.

Burtonelli would exit the limo first—his insistence. At least, if anyone wanted to put a bullet through his brain, they'd attempt it before his loved ones stood in the line of fire.

Hopefully, and good riddance, my asshole vindictive side whispered in my head.

The family would follow one by one, Cristian holding his mother's arm, the two daughters bringing up the rear. Greed would follow the judge into the event, and I would act as tail gunner, keeping everyone and everything within sight.

"Don't get out until I tell you it's clear," I told Burtonelli as the driver pulled up to the hotel's entrance.

He nodded his agreement, and I climbed from the limo, taking stock of our surroundings and the people waiting with cameras along the roped off area. I unbuttoned my suit coat, giving myself easy access to the gun in my shoulder holster.

Greed hurried from the lead car to take up position a few feet away, his focus on the area behind me as a handful of reporters flocked as close to the walkway as allowed.

Body tense, I motioned for Judge Burtonelli to climb out.

Light bulbs flashed as he straightened once out of the car, his wide grin and waves, the pointing finger he waggled at some, a true politician move. He strode up the carpet, and I nodded for Greed to follow on his heels, while I stood watch over the rest of the family. Mrs. Burtonelli exited next, Cristian and Marisa right behind her.

Giada's heel and smooth leg made an appearance, and I found my hand lowering, offering assistance when I hadn't done so for the other two ladies. Her fingers grazed mine—and twined as she appeared fully, lilacs and vanilla swarming my nose when she stood beside me.

Jaw clenched against the swell of my dick, I forced my focus on the crowd rather than her gaze I felt on my face.

"Thank you." The low words of appreciation jolted me to full fucking mast. My balls ached. My jaw ached.

I glanced down, intending to nod and look away, but her intense gaze snagged my attention.

A slow smile tilted her lips upward, her dimple appearing, and slammed me in the gut.

I stared as she started away, her fingers and gaze lingering on me until our hands stretched between us and she watched me over her shoulder.

Focus, Goddamnit.

Tearing my attention off Giada fucking hurt worse than a kick to the stomach, but I'd been paid to do a job, and I wasn't about to fuck up one of my best friend's reputation.

Fuck knew how long we would be in the judge's employ, and I hoped like hell we erased the threat to him sooner than later ... before I lost my damn mind over a woman and fucked up.

Warden counted on me.

The Burtonelli family counted on me.

I couldn't allow a single one of them to be our downfall.

2

GIADA

Father's new head of security was fine as fuck. Buzzed hair like a military man, his scruffy, cut jaw line and blue eyes sharp as a hawk. He watched me closely, sending lush shivers over my skin, and even though a "let's fuck all damn night long" spark had ignited between us the second our eyes had met, I felt he studied me for more than surface shit like most men did.

His steady gaze screamed intuition, and I swore empathy oozed from his pores, almost as obvious as the lust in his eyes. At least there hadn't been a hint of pity when I caught him looking at me during the limo ride while Father couldn't keep his hatred of me to himself.

Talk about embarrassing, but I didn't allow too

many emotions to show on my face. God knew
Father took advantage of every opportunity he could
seek out to belittle me—even in front of the damn
people he hired.

The fucktwat.

Father might be an asshole who'd decided I
would never measure up to his other two golden
children, but out of love for my mother and my baby
brother, I bit my tongue more often than not. I put
up with the unkind words in order to keep the peace,
but *some days,* especially when I hadn't gotten laid in
months and bitch from hell in need of a big dick
made an appearance...

I inhaled a deep breath, lifted my chin, and
walked the damn red carpet Father had insisted on
for a party he hadn't even planned.

Family. Loyalty.

Father saw them a bit differently than me, but we
believed in both whole-heartedly. The problem with
being born to people like my parents, I was expected
to *be* like them.

I'd been nothing but a disappointment, just like
Father often reminded me, the black sheep who
turned her fiery Italian temper and drive into
being *herself* rather than what everyone else
wanted.

Rebellion came easy. Feelings of adequacy and self-worth, not so much.

I was beautiful. Had a body women killed themselves for and men worshiped. I was even up and coming in the modeling industry, but I still felt like a failure deep inside where no one could see.

I'd hid it so well for so long ... but those arresting blue eyes of his seemed to see all the way through me.

He stood behind Father during dinner like a stoic sentinel, a mighty warrior with broad shoulders inside his dark gray suit. He didn't look at me as our meal progressed, his gaze flitting from one end of the ballroom to the other as though reading every single guests' intentions on their faces.

Logan Stone, a ninja warrior, according to Cristian.

"Isn't he hot?" Cristian had whispered in my ear as he'd hugged me earlier in my parent's foyer.

I'd known immediately who he'd meant. Not the pretty boy behind me—Greed, he'd called himself while seating me at our table—but the serious man who had towered over me in the doorway, whose mere brush of a glance down my body turned me on more than any man's hands had ever done in my twenty-six years.

He was hot as fuck, and I expected Cristian wanted to jump his bones just as badly as I did. Cristian didn't bother trying to hide his stares, though. Unashamedly open, emotions on his sleeve, my little brother salivated over our father's new head of security.

Hell, if Father ever learned of his only son's sexual orientation...

I couldn't even begin to imagine the backlash, the words, and the hurt he would experience.

My teeth clenched as I caught Father watching Cristian stare at Logan, his brow furrowing.

I swiped out my arm, knocked over my glass of champagne, some of it dripping onto my lap before soaking into the white linen table cloth. "Oops."

Father scowled fully, his attention once more upon me as I hopped out of my chair, drawing everyone's attention, too. Lips pursed, he wisely kept silent on whatever shit he grumbled in his head. If his supporters at the table with us knew the asshole side of him I was too-well acquainted with, he might lose some of his following. His contributions. His position of authority.

"If you'll excuse me," I said, grabbing my purse and moving out of a server's way to clean up my spill.

"Do you need help, dear?" Mother asked, putting her napkin onto the table and starting to rise.

"No." I offered a fake smile. "Stay and enjoy yourself. I'll be right back."

I made my way toward the bathroom, and felt rather than saw that a bodyguard shadowed me as I slipped out the double doors.

Logan, without a doubt, his gaze on my swaying ass.

I glanced over my shoulder to find my instincts spot on. Once in the quiet, carpeted hallway leading to the bathrooms, I stopped and waited for him to catch up.

His gaze fell to my face after scanning the immediate area.

"Giada," I said, offering my hand, "and if you so much as whisper to my father about how Cristian can't keep his eyes off you, I'll kick your ass."

The corner of his lips twitched, but his eyes remained cold as his last name as he gripped my hand. "Logan," he said, his rumbling voice slickening my pussy up good and ready for whatever he packed inside his slacks, "and if I hear your father say one goddamn word to Cristian about his attraction to men, I'll kick *his* ass."

My lips rose on their own as the connection I'd

felt between us in my parents' foyer thickened. "I think I like you, Logan Stone."

A good five seconds of silence lingered over us, thrumming my pulse before he answered. "I've got a job to do." His tone hinted at annoyance, and I lifted an eyebrow, allowing him to tug his hand from mine.

My gaze fell to his broad shoulders, and I imagined digging my nails into them as he planked above me. Thrusting ... fucking... "A little fun never hurt anyone."

"Too much fun can cause a shit ton of trouble."

"Not if you're smart about it." I inhaled deeply, stared up at him, trying like hell to read his face, see the attraction, the energy I could feel crackling between us. He smelled like a blustery fall day with a hint of manly musk beneath.

I wanted a taste.

My pussy wept over the emptiness plaguing it the previous couple of months since I'd told myself no fucking, no conquests—for my family's sake.

"As delicious as I imagine you'd taste," Logan said, leaning down to whisper in my ear and sending a rush of goosebumps over my skin, "as lush as you'd feel in my hands, I've got a job to do. Nothing and no one, no matter how gorgeous, is going to hinder me from completing my task."

Logan stepped back, hands clasped behind him as I struggled to slow down my heartbeat, stop the water works in my mouth and creaming between my thighs. Lips parted, I stared at him, my imagination a riotous mess of skin, lips, and teeth.

Mutual lust—but he was one stoic mother fucker.

"I'll change your mind," I said, more breathless than I would have liked, my pussy spasming with need for his dick.

"You won't."

Chin lifted, I glanced down over his tense form, noting the hard cock pressing against his left thigh. "We'll see." I flounced away, intent on dabbing at the champagne that had soaked into my dress—and tossing the panties his scent, his male *alpha-ness* had ruined.

I'd never met anyone like Logan Stone, and even though I expected Cristian would be heartbroken over me snagging his new love interest, I wasn't as stoic, didn't have the self-control to keep me from getting what I wanted.

And I wanted Father's head of security. I knew how to be sneaky, and with his occupation, I expected he did as well.

Logan didn't meet my gaze when I exited the

bathroom, but feeling his presence behind me as we moved back toward the ballroom, slickened my pussy once more.

I should have gotten myself off in the damn bathroom. Brow furrowed, I stepped back, allowing Logan to grasp the ballroom's door handle.

"Okay, little girl?"

I shot a glare at him. "Little?"

His lips twitched again.

"I have the female equivalent of blue balls, I'll have you know," I told him, my focus once more falling to the bulge in his pants. "And you've ruined my panties."

"Sorry to hear that." He pulled open the door but didn't seem the least bit contrite—or moved by my declaration.

"Stoic bastard," I muttered, striding past him. I swore I heard a chuckle, but my attention jerked toward the stage.

Father had taken to the podium, his voice booming in the speakers. A quick glance in my direction—with easily noted annoyance—and he continued on with his speech of thanks and all that bullshit, swaying the rich assholes in attendance to toss their dollars at his campaign manager.

I sat once more at the table that had been cleared

of china and crystal goblets, hands folded on my lap, a fake ass smile plastered on my face as I gave him my full attention all for the sake of my family.

He bragged about his accomplishments—Marisa's, too, praising her to high fucking heaven for following in his footsteps, while I fought to keep my faltering smile in place.

Marisa's cheeks flushed, and she glanced at me above the red roses and greenery center piece with the pity I'd come to loathe.

My return smile stated without words that all was well, when in truth, my chest felt like another knife stabbed deep, twisting.

Praise for Cristian came next—currently on track to become valedictorian of his class. He'd already been accepted to Harvard Law School, Father and Marisa's alma mater.

Mother squeezed my forearm, but I ignored her. She'd never done anything to stop Father other than quiet chides here and there when his abusive nature got out of control. She never once had stood up for me, sided with me, or backed my decision when I'd told them I planned to drop out of college.

Father started in on his campaign and bringing down the hammer on drug running through our state. While I appreciated his plan to clean up the streets, he'd only latched onto that issue when a few of his friends had gathered the year before to smoke their cigars and discuss politics after a long ass dinner I'd been ordered to attend.

The discussion had started at the table, and Father didn't bother hiding the calculating mind at work behind his eyes when the idea of running on the drug issue arose.

A great cause. A great desire—if it had been one in his heart rather than a means to a seat in the Senate. Unfortunately, by choosing such a stance, he'd made enemies, thus the need for amped-up security. If only his dogmatism came from a true desire for change...

I guzzled down two more glasses of champagne, becoming happily buzzed and no longer hurt by snide comments and distasteful glances by Father's peers. I didn't give a shit if they didn't like my sexy *Oscar de la Renta* gown or my past indiscretions. Fuck them and fuck their money. Perhaps it was time to cut my ties with my father—and pray I didn't lose the rest of my family in the aftermath.

Fucking the security guard would certainly set the stage for a blow out with Father, but I didn't want to hurt Logan or the security company he worked for. Sneaky, it would have to be ... and I would just have to find a different way to remove myself from the Judge Burtonelli picture.

———

"You will all be staying at the house until the threats have been nullified."

I stared at Father in the limo's dim interior, my drunken brain taking a few extra seconds to make out what he'd said. "What?" I asked, sure I hadn't heard right.

"You and Marisa are moving back in until I take my seat in the Senate."

I stared, seriously tempted to burst into laughter. The arrogance... I glanced at Mother to find her smiling.

"All of us back beneath the same roof. My babies."

I barely kept from snorting. She'd had too much to drink, too.

My focus didn't move back to Father as quickly as my head did. "I have a life outside of your campaign, Father."

"And you won't *have* a life at all if you're left unprotected!"

So maybe he cares a bit after all... I stared, sure I knew better.

"I won't have any scandal, any negative press from this family," he stated, his voice and gaze stern, "even if mourning is socially acceptable. I do *not* want that kind of spotlight on us."

The lightbulb went off in my buzzed head at the word scandal. Nope. He didn't care about my life—just his image.

I smiled tightly, feeling Logan's focus on my face. "And how long are we expected to move back in for?"

"The election is next November," he said with enough of a sneer I knew he questioned my intelligence.

I blamed the champagne for not remembering what he'd stated about staying until he took his seat in the Senate. Father continued to mutter under his breath about his drunk daughter's stupidity, but my heart lay dead in my damn chest as I stared out the window, the lights a blur in the darkness.

Living back at home. Every twenty-something's worst nightmare, especially when one parent was a narcistic prick and the other an enabler.

"My roof, my rules," Father continued, and I shut him out rather than hear what had been pounded into my brain years earlier. No drinking. No drugs. No partying when they left for an evening or weekend. No sleep overs of any sort—especially the opposite sex. No sex under their roof.

I glanced at Logan who radiated energy enough to flatten my damn father. Jaw clenched, he met my gaze, and I swallowed against sudden tightness in my throat. His pale blue eyes showed the type of caring, warmth, and protectiveness I would love to burrow inside. Hide away from the world.

Maybe have an orgasm or ten while entwining myself with him.

"Giada!"

I ripped my focus off Logan to meet my father's glare.

"Did you hear a word I just said or is your brain too sloshed by all that champagne you drank?"

I repeated verbatim when I expected he'd spewed—what I'd heard dozens of times before escaping the Burtonelli household three years earlier.

Lips pursed and dark eyes as cold as the night beyond the limo, he didn't blink until I finished.

"There will be no acts of indiscretion between now and November." His threatening tone, just like

LYNN BURKE

the promise of the belt back in the day, used to tingle my ass.

I nodded, smart enough to know, thank you very much, I had eleven months of hell ahead of me. At least my backside no longer felt his words in physical form. The last time I'd felt the lick of his belt had been when I was sixteen and he caught my then boyfriend trying to escape out my bedroom window.

"A hint—one whiff—of wrong choices that will result in bad press," Father continued, "and I'll send you to Italy."

A shudder rippled through me, pebbling my skin. A threat that would most definitely keep me in line if I hadn't already decided to somehow break away from the shadow of my father. My cousin in Italy was closer to Father's age than mine, and while I didn't usually mind the affection of my Italian heritage, he took it too far with his lingering hugs and wandering hands.

The first time I'd told Father that my cousin made me uncomfortable, he'd ripped me a new one, claiming I was making the tale up for attention.

Yeah. Fucktwat.

"I'll need clothes," I said, focusing on my mother, knowing she at least would agree with me on the smaller details of having my life turned upside down at my father's declaration.

"You can borrow a nightgown of mine for tonight," she said, still smiling. "Tomorrow, we'll have security escort you to your condo to pack up."

"Tomorrow is Christmas," I said, my voice as dead as the heart in my chest. I'd planned on spending the morning with friends and only returning to the Burtonelli house for the traditional family dinner I knew I wouldn't be able to put off.

"It'll be just perfect." Mother's eyes shown even though the haze of champagne probably muddled her vision, same as me. "Just like the old days," she breathed while beaming. "All my babies around the Christmas tree. We'll have cinnamon rolls and hot chocolate with miniature marshmallows."

Marisa smiled at Mother, the perfect little twit. Twenty-eight, happily married to Father's old firm, and having zero arguments about leaving her own condo behind. Cristian stared at Logan—still. A senior in high school whose best friend acted the beard to protect his ass from Father.

Sweet girl, but a sad situation since he would never be able to return her love. At least Cristian had such a friend. Nothing and no one had ever made attempts to shield me from Father's wrath.

We finally arrived at the house, and I lingered on my seat until everyone else exited before sliding toward the limo door, my head spinning more than I'd noticed at the party.

Logan's hand appeared same as it had when we'd arrived at the hotel, and I slipped my fingers through his, glancing up to offer my thanks as I swayed on my feet.

He tightened his hold, not that I had any plan of escaping him quickly. "Are you alright?" he murmured as Cristian hurried up the stairs to the front door.

"I might have had a bit too much to drink, but I'll be fine."

"That's not what I meant."

I forced a smile as our gazes collided once more, hating he'd seen and heard the embarrassment I constantly caused my father. "He can't hurt me."

Logan peered down at me, seeing straight through to my damn soul—I had no doubt. "Eleven months is a long fucking time."

I snorted, scanning the house's face and the flood of lights spilling from the windows. If only my child-hood home was actually filled with the comfort such light brought to darkness like the cold night wrapped around us. "No shit."

"Giada."

Warmth tingled between my thighs at his low murmur of my name, and I turned to find his stare on my lips. "Yes, Logan Stone?"

"My father was a bully of the worst sort."

"I'm sorry," I murmured, my own heart aching for him, for our shared pain.

"A lesser woman would have caved to your asshole of a father years ago."

Tears pricked my eyes. "I refuse to let him break me."

His slow smile lightened the heaviness in my heart and restarted the cream factory between my thighs. "I admire your strength. You've got balls, I'll give you that."

"Blue ones," I reminded him, an eyebrow raised in invitation.

"No indiscretions, I believe your father stated, and unlucky for you, I'm a rule follower."

"Fuck his rules." I trailed a fingertip down over his woolen coat's lapel, stepping closer. "There's no cameras inside the house. No one needs to know."

His jaw muscle ticked in the lights flooding from the house caressing the side of his face.

"Giada, dear!" Mother's voice carried from the

house, causing Logan's openness to shut down like a slamming metal door.

"I'll be right there," I called back to her, my attention riveted on the mask dropped into place over Logan's face.

He stepped away, releasing my hand. "I'm not going to fuck you under your father's roof."

"Hmm." I smirked. "But elsewhere?"

His gaze narrowed, and he leaned toward me once more. "If we'd met under different circumstances, Giada Burtonelli, I'd bare every inch of your skin, eat your pussy until you screamed, and bury my dick so deep inside your body you'd swear you died and went to heaven—and that would only be in the first hour."

Fuck. Yes.

My mouth dried up as I fought to come up with something besides falling to my knees and begging. I'd had my fair share of men over the years, but not a single one turned me on with mere words in the way Logan did.

"I'll need an escort to my condo tomorrow." My suggestion ticked that muscle in his sharp jaw again, but Greed approached us, ending our fun little conversation.

3

STONE

Greed's nudge to my arm tore my focus off Giada as she swayed her ass toward the house. That damn woman would be the death of me —or at least my ruination. Temptation beyond ice water after a good workout in my dojo.

"You going to take her up on the offer her eyes were shooting at you all night, or is she fair game?" Greed asked.

"Touch her," I told him, my tone hard, "and I'll bury your ass."

He chuckled but stepped out of my strike zone, opened hands raised. "Damn, man. Never seen you so worked up over a woman."

I slammed the limo door and knocked on the roof, letting the driver know he was good to put the car away in the three-stall garage. Turning my brain back on work, I glanced around the estate showing it much too dark for my liking. We'd already done a complete check on the security in place—and found it sorely lacking.

"She is fine as fuck, though," Greed said. "Can't argue that."

I shot a glare his way. "We're here to keep this family safe," I reminded him—and myself—none too kindly. "Warden's reputation is at stake, too. If you can't focus on the job, I'll have Warden can your ass and send over Sin."

"Sin's got a bum arm."

I clenched my teeth and started a perimeter walk around the house, my dick aching as much as my jaw. "We need some more flood lights out here," I tossed out before getting too far away Greed wouldn't hear me. "A few extra cameras, too."

"I'll make a note to get on it in the morning," he said while starting up the house's stairs.

Once I checked all the doors, I locked the front one behind me and set the house's alarm. Thankfully, the entire Burtonelli family had disappeared to the second floor.

Temptation gone, at least for night one.

First on watch, I told Green to catch some Z's and

made my way to the small closet-like security room Judge Burtonelli had set up a mere week earlier right off the foyer. Hastily installed cameras around the estate's exterior offered grainy images on a laptop provided by the home security company he'd hired to install the piece of shit.

I needed to get Devil, my computer whiz Viper brother, out the next day to get the place properly protected. With no interior cameras, I felt like we watched in the dark, unable to do my job to the best of my ability.

Not that I'd have been a fucking creep and watched Giada slip out of her dress and crawl between her sheets. Would she take up her mother's offer of a nightgown, or did she sleep naked?

Teeth once more clenched, I settled in for my shift. Christmas Eve and not a creature stirred, not even a mouse. Although my eyelids felt like sandpaper every time I blinked, I remained vigilant, watching the camera feeds. Quietly made my way around the lower level of the house when I needed to stay awake, peering out windows into the dark night.

One of Burtonelli's personal staff had the shit shift, relieving me in the middle of the night, and I made one last walk through of the house before closing myself in the guest room Mrs. Burtonelli had insisted I take in the east wing.

Greed had the room across the hallway. We would both stay on site, making a total of five full-time guards to watch over the family.

I already had Devil working to find the sender of the emailed "drop out of the Senate race by New Year's Eve, or we'll take you out ourselves" threat, but he'd yet to come up with any leads as to who might be behind them. My gut told me Arturo Martínez, the drug lord in control of New England, was the responsible party. Who else would feel threatened by Burtonelli's running?

Certainly not the little grunts who dealt beneath the cartel's radar. A dime a dozen, the local boys selling narcotics didn't have an empire to lose like Arturo did if Burtonelli landed the seat he ran for.

Fully clothed in the event I needed to act fast and one of the walkie-talkies on the bed stand, I finally collapsed on my bed for the foreseeable future. When I'd agreed to take on the Burtonelli job, I hadn't known we would be house guests more often than not. The idea of being all but married to the family twisted my gut.

The thought of being in close proximity with Giada Burtonelli swelled my dick.

Scowling, I rolled over, fought the need to grind against the mattress, punched the pillow, and closed my eyes.

The dojo would be fine without my daily appearance. Sensei Jason ran the kid's classes, and one of my kickboxing long-timers had agreed to take over the early morning fitness classes. A few hours a week in the office would keep things running as smoothly as they'd been going for over five years.

Being away from the motorcycle club and my Viper brothers would suck ass, though. In the club, I'd found the friendship and feeling of belonging I'd missed out on my whole life. Sure, most of the fuckers were royal bastards with violent streaks and lawless mindsets like other one-percenters, but they were *family*. The Vipers understood loyalty. Acceptances of differences. Having one's back in all things, at all times.

I'd been lucky to find my place within their ranks. If only Giada could find something similar. A supportive group to help her escape the prison of her name.

Claim her.

"Fuck," I muttered at the thought that slammed into my brain. I punched the pillow as my dick took interest yet again. "Got a fucking job to do."

Damn cock didn't give a shit, though, and I ended up stroking one out before my brain agreed to rest.

———

Christmas morning, and while I normally would be at the club with my brothers and their families, I found myself sitting in the security closet again, watching the house's exterior rather than the Burtonelli's drink their hot chocolate and eat cinnamon rolls around the huge tree in their family room.

Giada had come down the stairs in a light-colored robe, one that fell to mid-thigh, the top gaping enough to offer a nice view of cleavage. Bare-foot. Zero trace of makeup.

Still fucking hot as hell.

Tearing my focus off her didn't come easy, but the blood to my dick sure as fuck did.

I'd chosen another walk around the house—outdoors in the fucking cold—to talk myself down. A quick jerk off in the bathroom would have been better, but I refused to leave my post for something as selfish as release.

Shooting spunk into my hand sounded about as

satisfying as a kick to the balls. A warm, wet pussy would be fifty times better, but even the thought of one of the club whores getting me off curled my lip.

I wasn't a selfish man by nature, but the temptation to carry Giada away from her father, fuck the job, fuck the family, intensified every time I caught a hint of pain in her eyes.

Her pain fucking slayed me almost as much as her goddamn curves.

She eventually ended up in a too-tight outfit provided by her sister, and I had zero complaints to give, other than the ache in my balls over thoughts of sliding my dick between her lush tits.

My morning watch ended, and I readied to escape the Burtonelli household for a quick jaunt to the club to touch base with Devil about a new security system and enjoy some real holiday revelry for an hour or two.

Giada caught me before I could slip out the front door. "Hey."

Her low voice pulled me up short of reaching for the handle. I turned to find her smiling—the first I'd seen that morning—and a glint in her eye.

"The judge says I need a guard to accompany me to my condo to pack up some of my stuff."

Shit.

Three men watched the house, I planned an escape, and the fifth had finally sacked out after being up since three in the morning. I couldn't—wouldn't—send Greed or the other currently sitting in the closet with her, leaving only two guards on duty.

I was screwed.

"Get your coat," I said, pulling out my cell. A quick text to Greed let him know I had her in my care.

His damn wink emoji pissed me off, and I muttered inside my head until Giada returned in her tight ass jeans and the goddamn heels from the night before. At least she covered her tits with her winter coat, but fuck if the sight of her shapely calves wrapped in denim leading down to those fucking porn heels didn't turn me on.

Yeah. Hard-fucking-*on*.

"My truck," I told her as she sashayed past me through the front door I'd opened for her.

"Yes, sir."

I wasn't into kink beyond a bit of roughness, but her use of that damn word hit my groin like a shot of adrenaline. Thoughts of tying her down flitted through my too-active brain. Withholding her climax. Forced climaxes.

Fucking-A.

"Alright, big boy?" she asked as I settled into the driver side after seeing her into my truck.

"Just fine."

I managed two minutes of staying focused on the road before she shifted, a waft of lilacs drifting past my nose. A quick glance across the cab showed her gaze plastered to my face.

"What?" I asked, turning back to the road.

"How'd you escape him?"

"My dad?"

"Yeah."

I glanced in my side mirror and turned on my blinker to pass the slow fucker in front of me. "He said 'for your own good' one too many times."

Giada made a sound of disgust. "One of my father's favorites as well."

"I was eighteen," I said, not wanting to dwell on the fucker I'd been hired to protect. "Just earned my black belt in karate, and Pop being the military asshole he was, decided to test me on his own. I'd chosen to only block his fists throughout the years, but sprawling on the floor with blood running from my nose that day... Yeah. He spit on me, told me he'd done it for my own damn good. I decided it was an affair of honor, just like the creed I'd been saying for years."

"Tell me you stood up and kicked his ass."

"I put him down with three punches."

"Good for you."

I glanced over at Giada to find her smirking. "Best day of my life," I said, turning forward once more, that sense of power I'd felt simmering inside me returning, "but also the worst since I left my mom and younger sister behind."

"Do you have any contact with them?"

"Mom texts me on my birthday every year, but that's it. My sister was always a daddy's girl—he couldn't do any wrong in her eyes. Sure, I miss her, but I had a clear conscious leaving her behind. Knew Pop wouldn't hurt her. Ever."

Giada let out a sigh. "I can't leave Cristian alone."

I nodded, not sure if she saw, but kept quiet while she told me about the baby brother she'd lay her life down for. A beard for a girlfriend, deep in the closet even from their mom, with Marisa none the wiser, either.

"If Father ever found out..." She let out a heavy sigh.

My GPS told me we'd arrived at our destination, and I parked around the back of her condo building, checking out the lack of people or activity in the surrounding area.

"When will Cristian be eighteen?"

"He already is, but he'll never leave. He has every intention of going to Harvard Law School, working alongside Marisa, and settling down with a lovely young lady someday."

"Why?"

"Because it's expected of him."

"Well that's a fucking shame."

"Tell me about it."

I turned off my truck and tipped my head toward the building's rear entrance. "I want you in front of me—don't stop for anyone or anything."

"Yes, sir."

Once more biting back a groan, I slipped out of my truck and rounded the hood, my attention scanning non-stop as Giada climbed out to join me in the cold. Not that I really expected an attempt on her life, but I kept close watch—not on her ass surprisingly—until locked inside her condo.

I made her stay by the front door while I did a quick sweep of all five rooms, and finding the place empty of bodies but our own, returned to find her coat in hand, her tits perky as fuck.

Ripping my focus off her chest, I shed my own

coat and tossed it over the back of the couch. "Pack up what you need. I have a call to make."

She sashayed back down the hallway, and I did watch, drinking my fill of her round ass and those goddamn heels. At her pause in the bedroom doorway, I lifted my gaze upward to find her smirking at me over her shoulder.

"See something you like?" she asked in that low tone that kicked a grunt from my chest.

"Pack."

Giada sniffed and disappeared, and I adjusted my dick before walking to the window overlooking the back parking lot.

Rather than follow after her, toss her on her bed, and bury my face between her ass cheeks, I pulled out my cell and called Devil, giving him a job to do on Christmas day.

4

GIADA

Logan had the self-control of a saint. I knew what Marisa's jeans did to my ass. I also knew what my spiked heels did to a man's brain and balls. The look in his eyes when I'd glanced back to find him watching me creamed my panties—conservative ones I also had to borrow from Marisa.

I caught the low tone of his voice from the living room, and realized he must have made the call he'd said he needed to place. While tossing a week's worth of clothes into a bag, I couldn't get my mind off Logan and the connection we had—beyond sexual, sharing a bond of abusive pain.

Father hadn't spared the rod when I'd been a wild child, but he'd ceased with the physical punishments after that event with the ex-boyfriend and the window, thank God. At that point, I'd lost privileges for my misbehaving. Having electronics taken away hurt more than the stinging pain of his belt.

Not having a means of mental escape sucked ass. I'd grown to love books in a major way. Went so far as to have a stack on my bed stand compliments of the local library. I'd started with mild YA coming of age stories which bloomed into NA romances. Unfortunately, the library didn't carry heat beyond romancelandia's queen, Ms. Roberts herself, but she'd packed enough heat to hook me on the naughty whenever I managed to sneak my e-reader once Father went to bed.

I grabbed the new e-reader I'd bought myself for an early Christmas present and vibrator from my bed stand, expecting I'd be putting both to good use unless I could get Logan to share what swelled the front of his jeans.

The man looked hung—and I sure as hell wanted to find out the length and girth for myself.

Whatever conversation he'd been having ended, and I considered my wardrobe for the rest of the day ... or at least the next hour or so.

After showering.

I finally took off my heels and peeled off Marisa's jeans, listening and hoping to hear Logan's footfalls in the hallway that led to my open bedroom door.

No such luck.

Shirt and bra slung toward my hamper, I grabbed up some new clothes and peeked out the door toward the living room. Logan stood by the window, his focus outside, but his brow smooth, indicating nothing threatening lingered beyond.

Biting back my smirk, I straightened and started across the hallway toward the bathroom. "I'm taking a shower," I said without glancing his way.

The resulting groan from the living room widened my grin as I disappeared into the bathroom. He'd gotten an eyeful, alright.

Now *maybe I'll get lucky.*

No such fucking luck, even though I took my good old time, shaving the bits and rubbing my lotion all over my body once finished—with the door wide open in invitation.

I finally pulled on the lacy thong and long-sleeve t-shirt I'd brought along into the bathroom. The shirt had three buttons on the low scoop neck, but I unsnapped them all and turned sideways to check myself out in the full-length behind the bathroom door. Just see-through enough, the shirt clung to my chest, offering a hint of areola around my hardened nipples, and fell to the tops of my thighs.

Being in front of cameras for the previous three years made walking around half naked easy, even if my heart pounded and pussy threatened to soak the bit of lace between my thighs.

Hair wet and hanging to my shoulders, I moved down the hallway—no sign of Logan.

He came into view in my periphery as I entered the condo's main living area, off to the right and around the corner—where he wouldn't have seen me if I'd decided to waltz back across the hallway again without a stitch of clothing on.

"Coffee?" I asked, smirking as I turned my back on him in the kitchen.

Logan muttered a few curses under his breath. "Yeah," he finally answered, his voice ragged and pussy-tingling.

Panties ruined.

He made no complaint over my lack of decent clothing as I set the coffee pot to brewing, but he also didn't move from his spot, his stare licking at my backside like blazing flames.

The perking started up, and I finally turned to find him gripping the chair's arms, his knuckles white, his eyes on me with a heated gaze that slid down over my front and back up. Goosebumps rose over my skin, tightening my nipples even harder.

My insides quaked, leaving me breathless. "Tempted to ... what did you say last night? Bare every inch of my skin, eat my pussy until I scream, and bury your dick so deep inside my body I'd swear I'd died and gone to heaven?"

His throat moved as he swallowed—the first break in the stoic façade of his face. He couldn't seem to find his voice, so I closed the distance between us, my pulse thrumming like mad.

Three feet in front of his spread legs, and I stopped, my tongue wetting my lower lip at the sight of the hard length swelled against his left thigh.

He swore again, but didn't so much as twitch his fingers or his focus off my chest.

I tugged the hem of my shirt down, the drag of soft cotton over my nipples bringing a moan to my lips. My girls already threatened to pop out of the low neckline, so I helped them along until cool air nipped at my hard nubs.

"Christ, Giada."

I lifted my breasts together, and he groaned—but didn't make a move to take me up on my offering.

Fine. Plan B.

I lowered onto his lap, pressed tight against his groin, my hands going to the back of his head, my fingernails scraping along his short hair. "Touch me, Logan."

"Fucking-A." His hands closed over my ass cheeks, and he yanked me tighter against his hardness. "Goddamn temptress from *fucking* hell—"

His voice cut off as he closed his mouth over my nipple, and I gasped, my eyelids falling shut as his deep pull shot straight to my clit.

"God," I gasped again as his teeth scraped and fingers dug into the flesh of my ass. My hips moved in time with his thrusts against me, his mouth leaving my nipple to suck and bite the soft flesh surrounding it, without doubt, marking my skin.

The thought thrilled me, but I wanted more.

I grabbed his chin and lifted his head without resistance. Our mouths met with a clash of teeth and tongue, my whimpers lost to the buzzing in my ears. All thought obliterated as his breath stole mine, the sweetness of his taste flooded my senses, the hardness of his body beneath me sending a rush of need through me.

Still not enough.

Reaching between us soaked the back of my

hand on my own arousal that leaked through my thong, but I found his hard cock trapped inside his jeans.

He hissed against my lips as I squeezed. "Greedy little girl."

"Yes," I agreed with a whisper, shifting back as he allowed me better access to the snap of his jeans.

"Fuck, I don't want to do this."

I lifted my focus to his face, to find him watching my fingers on his zipper. "Tell me to stop."

"Can't." His jaw clenched, and he met my gaze.

I slowly slid down the zipper and reached inside —commando. My lower lip caught between my teeth as I grasped his cock.

Logan's head tipped back against the chair, his throat working again, but he held my stare. "Take it out."

I did as told, his hands a vise grip on my ass. Fuck, he was big. I glanced down to find his girth kept my fingertips from closing around him. Pre-cum oozed from the tip, and I swiped over it, coating my palm for a long, downward stroke.

"Fuck." He lifted his hips, cursing again as I slid my hand back upward for another swipe over the leaking head.

My lips parted—and he yanked me close, sealing his mouth over mine, one hand tangling in my hair, the other yanking my working hand from his cock and twisting that arm behind my back to hold me tight against his front.

The soaked lace of my panties lay between us, slick and hot, creating the perfect texture to rub against my clit as he thrust the back of his cock against me.

I whimpered. Shivered and shook—no man had brought me to climax in such a way, but tingles rose in my toes—impending explosion on its way.

A shudder rippled through me, and I pulled away from his mouth to cry out, the blinding white light of my climax bursting behind my clenched eyelids. He latched onto my throat and sucked, his thrusts across my clit continuing until I sagged against him.

I blinked, and found my back pressing into the couch across from where we'd been, Logan straddling me, one foot on the floor, his other knee on the couch.

"Hold your tits together," he said with a grunt while working his huge cock.

I lifted and pressed them together as told, my

pulse still thundering, trying to catch my breath from the most earth-shattering orgasm of my damn life.

He held the base of his cock and slid between my breasts with a groan.

I lifted the girls higher, and he moved with me, shoving the head close enough to my mouth my flicking tongue caught a taste of his salty pre-cum.

"Fuck, Giada." He grasped my head, holding me upward, and fucked my tits, gifting me with a taste— sometimes an inch or two between my opened lips.

He panted. I panted, my pussy so damn achy and wet I rubbed my thighs together hoping to get myself off again when he finally released.

"Give it to me," I whispered up at him as he fucked my girls, his blue eyes hooded and lust-filled. "I want your cum all over my face. My tits."

He growled and shoved forward, his thick cock sliding in ... deep ... choking as I let go of my breasts and grabbed his ass.

I struggled to accommodate his girth as he fucked my face, salivating and tears rolling down my face, but I held tight, taking all he gave, desperate for more.

"Gonna come so fucking hard," he growled

through clenched teeth, his fingers yanking on my hair.

"Mmm," I egged him on around my mouthful until he choked me again.

"Swallow."

Heat shot into the back of my throat, and I swallowed around his cock, moaning and whimpering as he backed out and jerked another few spurts across my chin and breasts.

I reached between my thighs to ease the ache, the emptiness, but he grabbed my wrist.

"No." He scooted down, slipped off my panties, and nosed my thighs apart.

A hiss escaped me at the first slow lick of his tongue from my asshole to my clit. Another as he grasped my thighs with bruising fingertips and opened me wide.

"So fucking pretty."

My eyelids fluttered open.

He stared at my pussy—and dove in with teeth and tongue.

I came undone again, trying to bring my thighs together against his head while convulsing with my climax, but he held me open, lapping at my cum, making sexy as fuck noises deep in his throat.

He shoved two fingers deep inside my pulsing

passage, rubbing roughened pads against my g-spot. Another climax shot through me before the second ended, and I bowed on the couch, my fingernails digging into his scalp as he wrecked me.

Ruined me—without even fucking me.

His thrusting fingers slowed, and my legs went lax in his hold as I fought to catch my breath. Heat flushed my skin, dampness on my forehead, the stickiness of his cum on my face and breasts cooling.

"I could eat this pussy all damn day," he mumbled against my lower lips while sliding his fingers from my body.

I shuddered a sigh as he licked me clean, the flick of his tongue across my sensitive clit jerking me where I sprawled, boneless.

"Fucking delicious."

He stood, and I watched through heavy eyelids as he pushed down his jeans, kicking off his shoes. Off came the shirt, and my mouth flooded with drool.

Holy mother Mary of *fucking* god, he was ripped. I drank in the sight of his thick pecs, the damn eight-pack rippling down his core. The lush V of his cut hips, the long length of him hanging flooded my mouth with drool again.

"Goddamn," I groaned my appreciation, "you're one fine specimen of a man."

"And you're a fucking goddess." Logan swept me up off the couch, and I wrapped my trembling legs around his waist.

I nibbled on his chin, licked the scruff along his jaw as he carried me to the bathroom, his cum smearing between our chests.

"Goddamnit, woman, you turn me into a teenager who can't think with the head he ought to."

I buried my snicker in his warm neck. "Good."

He set me on my feet, but sprawled a palm on my ass cheek to keep me pressed against him while he used his other hand to turn on the shower. His hold felt possessive, sending flutters through my belly.

To be owned by such a man ... I'd never grow bored. Never get enough.

"Get in." He released me and stepped back, and I frowned as he turned and left me alone.

"Where are you off to?" I shot out, happy to not sound like a whiny little bitch.

"Checking the locks and out the windows one last time before I fuck you against the shower wall!"

Oh God.

I swallowed and hopped in, putting my whole head under the spray to rinse off his cum before turning to face the spray, eyes closed, my mind on a racing collision course with what I hoped was my destiny.

He entered silently behind me, his hands on my waist bringing a squeal to my lips, his musky scent weakening my knees. "Bend over." His hot breath on my ear sent shivers through my body.

I bent without hesitation or complaint, the spray hitting me in the middle of my back as I arched like a pussy cat in heat.

Logan grasped my ass cheeks and spread me open, and I shuddered as his tongue rimmed the hole no man had breached.

"Oh, holy *hell*." I groaned as he shoved his tongue inside me, his hand cupping my pussy.

A groan rumbled in his chest as he ate my ass, his fingertips playing with my clit, my swollen lower lips—rimming my quivering pussy. He brought back the ache deep inside me with a vengeance, until I trembled to stay upright, gasping and whimpering, my head hanging low, water dripping from my hair and the tip of my nose and eyelashes.

"I want your cock inside me," I said on a half-sob, so far gone with need I couldn't think straight.

Logan yanked me upward, his hard length

gliding between my thighs, one hand in my hair, the other grasping at one of my heaving breasts.

"I want to fuck you bare, Giada—tell me I can."

"I-I'm on the pill," I managed to gasp as he bit down where my neck meets my shoulder.

"Clean?"

"Yes."

"Me, too." He lifted me to my tiptoes with his hold on my chest, bent his knees, and I arched my back, pressing my ass back—offering my pussy.

He notched. Paused.

"Please—"

He thrust deep with a grunt, ripping a shriek from my lungs.

Huge. Goddamn, fucking *huge.*

A slow glide out, and he shoved back in, filling me so damn full, I couldn't catch my breath. Didn't want to.

"So perfect." Another slow pull out and thrust. "So tight around my dick, Giada. So. Fucking. Perfect." He rolled my nipple between his fingers while thrusting up into me, his forearm and elbow keeping me tight against his hard as hell body.

He bit my ear. "Put your foot up on the tub's edge."

Panting, I lifted my leg, opening me up. He took

advantage of the better angle by once more bending his knees, and slammed into my cervix.

"Fuck!" I fell forward, palms on the tile again as he grasped my hips, pumping in and out of me with steady drags against my grasping inner walls. My ass jiggled as he slammed into me over and over, his grunts and curses as much a turn on as his bruising fingertips and plundering cock.

This is what it feels like to be owned.

I'd read all about alphas claiming women, but to feel it—to taste the lust, to hear the animalistic sounds swirling with the rising steam...

Heaven. I'd died and gone to heaven just like he'd promised.

I came—hard—without a touch to my clit, without a pinch to my nipples. Four times in one goddamn day.

"God, Logan..." I groaned his name a second time, waiting for his cum to shoot deep inside me, but he pulled out and lifted me into his arms.

A limp noodle, I rested my back on the cold tile as he thrust into my pussy once more. My legs somehow found their way around his waist, ankles crossing to keep me in place as he plowed into me, his mouth taking mine in a frantic kiss.

"Come around me, Giada," he said against my

lips, thrusting and grunting. "Need to feel you pull me deeper."

"C-can't."

Logan grasped my ass cheeks and squeezed, his upper body holding me tight against the shower wall. "Please, baby ... please. Need to feel you let go when I come inside you."

His fingertip found my asshole and rimmed, catching my breath.

"Like that?" he gasped out while burying deep once more.

Moaning, I managed to nod.

"Look at me."

I forced my eyelids open as he stilled, our bodies twined tight. Pale blue fire filled his eyes, catching me up in a whorl of flaming need.

He worked his fingertip inside my ass, and I writhed in his hold, need rising up to choke me as he slid deeper.

A mere finger, but I felt full to bursting between that and his dick shoved up against my womb.

He brushed his lips over mine as I panted, his slow drag out of my pussy making my eyes want to roll back into my head. "Come for me, baby." His fingertip rubbed inside my ass, and he shoved his cock back in with a grunt.

My pussy clamped down on him, and he swallowed my cries, bucking into me, drawing out my climax yet again. One last deep thrust, and his cock jerked, heat erupting, spurting deep inside.

Beyond done.

Fucking obliterated.

5

STONE

y dick spurted one last time inside heaven, and before two seconds passed, I cursed myself. My lack of control. My giving into temptation like a goddamn horny punk who couldn't keep his dick inside his pants.

I fucking knew better.

Even though my usual spidey-sense lay quiet in the back of my brain, promising safety to the one I'd been hired to protect, I couldn't help but feel like a damn failure.

Warden was going to kill me.

So was Giada's dad—if the judge ever found out I'd stuck my finger up his daughter's ass and fucked her young pussy.

No way to hide the lust between us, though. Yeah, we'd slaked it for a time, I knew while lifting my head to study the gorgeous face inches from mine, but I'd be back on her like a front snap kick given the shot.

Her dark lashes fluttered and lifted, her satisfied, sleepy green eyes knifing my gut.

I'd known Giada less than twenty-four hours, and I was dead gone on the woman.

The fuck have I done?

"Don't shut down on me," she whispered while tightening her legs around my waist and grasping my face in her hands. "Don't you *dare* shut me out, Logan Stone."

"Kinda hard to do with my dick buried inside your tight pussy."

Fuck, I needed to lift her off me and get her back to her parents.

"I like your dick buried inside me."

I groaned and tipped my forehead against hers. "What I just did shouldn't have happened."

"What *we* just did certainly *should* have," she countered, her tone biting. "I wanted you, you wanted me. How can that be wrong?"

"Because you're my *job*, Giada."

She pushed my face away from hers, a scowl

denting her brow and fire lighting in her eyes. "I'm more than a fucking job."

"Shit." Her fire turned me the fuck on, and my semi took an interest in the warmth still cradling it. "Goddamn right you are—and that's the problem."

One of her eyebrows arched. "How so?"

I studied her eyes, the smooth skin above her brows, achingly gorgeous high cheekbones on either side of a perfectly straight nose. Full fuckable lips swollen and red from my mouth.

I didn't do relationships. Didn't allow anyone inside where they might manipulate and destroy the fortress I'd built up after years of laboring to rid my head and heart of the abuse my father had laid on me.

Would she understand?

"You're scared." Her words hit the goddamn nail on the head before I could vocalize my thoughts.

"Yeah."

Her slow smile soothed me as much as the tender caress of her thumbs along my jaw as she continued to cradle my face in her hands. "I don't let anyone inside, either, Logan. Life's easier that way, isn't it?"

I leaned in and kissed her, showing her what I

felt had sprouted inside my soul, the connection I felt between us. She sighed and melted into me.

My mind warred as the water spitting from the shower head grew cold, and neither of us spoke while finally climbing out and drying off.

While I'd have loved to collapse on her bed and pass the fuck out, I still had a job to do—and Devil to meet back at the judge's house to amp-up the security system.

Giada followed me into the living room where I grabbed my cell and glanced out her windows again.

Greed had texted to let me know all was quiet.

Devil had also sent a message he was on his way —earlier than I'd expected.

"Shit." I grabbed my jeans off the floor.

"What's wrong?"

"We gotta get back."

She let out a sigh, but turned away.

I watched her go while tugging up my jeans over still-damp legs. A fluffy towel was wrapped around her body, but it couldn't hide the curves I knew would haunt me for the rest of my goddamn life.

———

We should have talked on the way back to her parents, but I couldn't find the fucking words. Giada peered out the passenger window, her brow slightly furrowed as though deep in thought.

I told myself fucking her had been a mistake since it went against the lines I drew about getting involved with people I protected. I told myself I knew better, that I should have been stronger.

Pop's voice echoed in my ear, something I hadn't heard for a long fucking time. Failure. Letting people down. Not good enough. A loser. One wrong choice brought it all back to fuck with my head.

The only reason I'd caved beyond her being too much of a temptation was the fact we'd been closed up in her condo, secure, away from the man whose life had been threatened. While whoever it was wanted the judge out of the race "or else", not once was the Burtonelli family itself mentioned.

But I'd been a patched member of the Vipers long enough to know that when an ultimatum got slapped down onto the table, it didn't matter who stood in the way. Innocent casualties happened. Manipulation by hurting loved ones occurred.

Bad men would do anything to get what they wanted—to win.

While I didn't necessarily put myself in that category like some of my brothers, I strove to excel—in all things, beyond the physical as well. And allowing my guard to lower to enjoy a piece of ass...

She's more than a piece of ass, you stupid fuck.

I knew it—she had to know it. The damn connection between us popped and sizzled from close proximity alone. Just the scent of her filling the cab of my truck, the energy radiating off her soft skin mere feet away kept my dick in a constant state of chub.

Unable to help myself, I glanced her way while slowing at the Burtonelli residence gate. Her shoulders wilted in on themselves, and she let out a sigh.

"Giada."

She turned. "Yeah?"

"Don't let him get to you."

"He will. Always does."

A muscle in my jaw ticked and I stopped in front of the gate. Rather than put the window down to buzz us in, I turned fully to look at her.

"I'm going to have one hell of a time keeping my mouth shut whenever he starts in on you," I said.

"You have to, otherwise you'll be gone. Father doesn't take lightly to people telling him what to do."

I nodded. "Can't do that to Warden. He's my brother."

"I thought you only had a sister?"

"Brother as in Viper brother. Not blood."

One of her eyebrows arched. "Viper as in the vicious ones?"

"Yep. Been a patched member for over ten years."

"Shit." She snickered. "No wonder you're an alpha asshole."

I frowned. "I'm not an asshole."

"Not really." Her dimples kicked me in the gut. "It's an MC romance thing—all readers are hot for that shit."

My turn to arch a brow. "MC romance thing?"

She winked. "You're better than the stories, Logan Stone, and we're nowhere near done with our own."

Our own ... as though we had a story, a future ahead of us. "We can't continue this, Giada."

"Like hell we can't." She straightened, the fire lighting in her eyes, giving her the backbone she'd been missing minutes earlier. "I'm not about to give up the first man to look at me like you do."

"How's that?"

Her scowl faded, and the sincerity growing in her eyes meant more to me than happiness in that moment. "Like I have worth."

I felt the need to swallow against the sudden

emotion that came out of left fucking field. "You do have worth—don't let that fucker of a father tell you any different. You're strong. Independent. You've got enough spunk to fuel ten women. Don't let him kill it, don't let him beat you down. In eleven months, he'll either be Senator or not. You'll be free to move on with your life—for good."

"Will you be there?" Zero trace of manipulation lay in her tone, just pure inquiry and hope.

I stood on a fucking cliff, wanting to leap off yet wanting to shield myself from the unknown, the spooky as shit possibilities of a future I couldn't see.

"I'll be there." A three-worded answer, fucking loaded.

A glint lit in her eye as she smirked. "Then let's go face the fire. I can take it if you can."

Stomach in knots, I put down my window and buzzed the intercom. I had no doubts she could take it—but the desire to protect not just her body but her mind would test me beyond what I'd ever known.

Of that, I had zero fucking doubt.

6

GIADA

Logan's Viper brother Adrian, aka Devil, waited in the foyer when we arrived, a computer bag over his shoulder. He was handsome as a devil, too, all clean-shaven with brown bedroom eyes and lashes to kill for.

His quick once over down my body and back up brought a growl to Logan's chest, and I bit back a smirk.

"Like that, is it?" Devil asked, not bothering to hide his amusement while meeting Logan's stare.

"Yep."

"Gotcha, brother." Devil didn't spare me another glance, but started in on computer lingo, security cameras, and stuff I had no interest in.

A shiver licked over my skin as every motorcycle

gang romance I'd ever read with similar happenings over a woman and a patched member's response trickled through my head.

Unspoken claiming?

Holy shit, yes, and then some please.

Butterflies jammed to the bass thump of my heart as I stared up at Logan. I could fall for him—hard. The L word and all, given the opportunity and time. He said he would be there, and I knew I sure as hell wanted it.

And Father would be livid. I would once again be labeled the disappointment of the family. The selfish girl who always put herself above the needs and best interests of the family.

My throat tightened—and Logan diverted his attention to me for a brief second as though he felt my sudden pain, his brow furrowing.

"You alright?"

Unable to speak, I nodded and tried to smile.

One of the house's staff came from outside, two of my bags in hand, bringing along with him a blast of cold air—and reality.

I was back in prison, and the tantalizing man I decided I wanted more than oxygen had to protect the one man who could easily ruin me for life. Father could kick me out on my ass, keep the rest of my family from seeing me. His threats would easily keep Cristian, Marisa, and Mother in line.

He would rule them with fear.

And while I could care less about the inheritance I would miss out on, I would be without family.

Cristian had to make an appearance at that second, sauntering in from the living room. His face flushed as he noticed Logan first, but he ripped his attention off him and caught my eye.

"Hey, Sis."

My smile came easier. "Hey, kiddo."

"I ate the last cinnamon roll."

"Jerk."

His grin and double dimples made him the cutest damn thing in the world. My baby brother, pretty much the love of my life. I grabbed him and hugged him hard, never wanting to let go.

"Love you," I whispered, knowing I could never cross father—couldn't ever lose my loved ones.

"Tell me you got a taste."

I pulled back, my face hot. "Cristian Burtonelli!"

"Well?" He quirked a brow, and glanced at Logan who had gone back to conversing with Devil as they moved farther into the house.

I bit my lip, not wanting to lie, but not wanting to hurt my brother's feelings.

He turned his focus back on me as Logan and Devil disappeared down the hallway. "I'll only ever live the life I want vicariously, Giada, so don't hold back the truth if you think it'll hurt," he whispered.

I grasped his face in my hands, too overcome for words. A kiss to his forehead and another hug came easy. Getting out a description about my time with Logan proved impossible through the tightness in my throat.

"He hurt you?" Cristian asked, his Italian temper peeking through as I pulled back, my pain probably obvious on my face.

"No," I managed with a wobbly smile.

Cristian's eyes lightened as his dimples appeared again. "You're head over heels. Damn." He whistled. "Never thought I'd see the day a man would wrap the 'variety is the spice of life' girl around his little finger."

I shrugged, huffing with a bit of laughter.

"That good, huh?"

"Better than good."

"Damn. You gotta tell it all, Sis. Every last damn detail—I want it all. Merry Christmas to me."

"You're too young and innocent to hear it all."

"Bullshit." He grasped my hand and pulled me toward the stairs. "I might hide in the closet," he whispered back at me, "but there's others in there with me sometimes."

I laughed outright at his wink. "You little sneak!"

"You have *no* idea."

"Do tell."

"You first."

A newfound connection between me and the love of my life—like hell would I ever jeopardize that. Heart aching but mind set in granite, I locked myself in my old childhood bedroom and unpacked while spilling secrets with my baby brother who I accepted wasn't so little anymore.

7

STONE

I sat brooding at a table surrounded by my Viper brothers, nursing a beer, my mind battling against the craziness in the club around me. Christmas music blasted, rug rats shrieked while playing tag around us, and dozens of conversations buzzed from one end of the club to the other.

A huge ass tree lit up one corner, wrapping paper and toys littering the area around it. The scent of turkey and ham still clung to the air, the leftovers I'd devoured from the early afternoon meal settled pleasantly in my stomach.

I couldn't get Giada out of my head. I'd been able to avoid her and the possibility of a run-in with her father, every minute of the afternoon and early evening taken up by Devil and updating their security system. Feeling ten times better about what we'd set into place, I'd slipped away like a true asshole she'd claimed me to be, no goodbye, no see ya later.

Warden sat beside me, Shaun straddling him, their faces close while they smiled and chatted in their own little world.

Ryker, our sergeant at arms, sat across from me, arms crossed and scowling as always, his hazel eyes cold as fuck, the dome of his shaved head lit by an overhead light. Vigil, our president, sat to his right, elbows on the table as he peered around him to chat with Sin, aka Dustin Murphy, whose arm was still tucked tight to his body with a sling.

Vigil's brother and our VP Ricky, who, like Ryker, preferred his own name, lounged between me and his brother. The two could easily pass for twins with their auburn-tinted hair, clipped beards, and pale eyes. But unlike Vigil with his booming voice, Ricky was a quiet one and scowled just as much as Ryker. Broody bastards, both of them.

While Devil would have normally sat with us, he'd stayed behind at the Burtonelli's with Greed to teach him the system we'd set up that afternoon.

Darkness had long since fallen as we bullshitted rather than focus on any club business.

The married patched members with kids were the first to head out, their kids still on a sugar high and loud as hell. Other couples slowly disappeared, leaving a handful of prospects, our table, and a few other Vipers who didn't have families of their own to head off with.

Two club whores still hung around, trying to lighten the moods of those soured by holiday festivities but must not have anything else or any other place to be.

"Turn the fucking music down!" Vigil hollered to the prospect behind the bar once the last kid's ass disappeared through the door. "Fucking same Christmas shit over and over," he continued to grumble while turning back to our table. "Thank fuck it's over."

"Grinch," his brother muttered before sipping his whiskey.

"Fuck off, Ricky." Vigil sat back and crossed his arms, his frown on Warden and the hot little number grinding on his lap. "Why don't you go get us all a round of drinks, little girl?" he told Shaun.

"Sure thing." She hopped off Warden's lap, and he slapped her ass while adjusting his dick.

Jealousy—and loneliness—snaked through me, and I focused on my president rather than Warden who watched Shaun saunter away, so much damn emotion in his eyes even *my* heart ached.

They hadn't been together long, but there was no question they belonged together. He'd known Shaun since she'd been born—literally having been in the hospital with her father and mother when she'd given birth.

Warden had been her father's best friend, her protector, and even though tragedy and blame tore the friends apart, Shaun's father had trusted Warden to watch over her when he decided to take on the cartel in retaliation for attempting to take him out.

Ben Thode, one of Boston's kingpins found his demise, but his daughter and heir found the love of her life. She also had gone a bit overboard with Christmas, buying every single one of the members' kids gifts as well as gifting something to the men sitting at the table with me.

She'd joked when handing out the envelopes with a few, crisp Franklins each, that she wanted us to use the cash to wine and dine the next woman to snag our attention. Since she'd made Warden the happiest man on the earth—which he'd agreed to when she'd winked at him—she hoped we all would find the same.

Well, I'd found a woman I sure as fuck wanted to

claim, but I wasn't about to share that shit with my brothers and reap the consequences. I enjoyed my job working for my best friend—even though I didn't really need it. The dojo kept my head above water just fine.

My cell vibrated in my back pocket, and I fished it out.

Devil: **Got the answer we've been waiting on.**

I waited, watching the dots blink.

Devil: **Arturo. Just like we'd expected.**

"Fuck."

He still in Columbia? I shot back.

Devil: **Yep. Heading home now. We'll catch up later.**

I scrubbed a hand down over my face and shoved my cell back in my pocket, wishing for and yet knowing the Burtonellis weren't any safer with the cartel leader's location. That fucker had the contacts and cash to be halfway around the world when a bullet or bomb took out the wannabe senator set on eradicating the cartel's business from New England.

Five sets of eyes peered at me as I looked up.

"Arturo's the one who sent the death threats to Burtonelli," I shared the news.

A few curses sounded, but Vigil kept silent, his

focus sliding to Warden. "Exactly as we'd thought. What do you want to do about it?"

Warden wasn't one to make a rash decision. His beard twitched as though he clenched his jaw a time or two while considering. "Burtonelli hired me and my boys to keep him safe, not do away with the threat—even though I'd love to bury the fucker."

Arturo had kidnapped Shaun the week before, and even though we'd managed to get her back through threat alone, we'd all known the shit would eventually hit the damn fan.

"I say we make plans to take the fucker out," Ryker said, his steady stare at Vigil revealing his surety the Vipers could easily pull it off. "Lop the head off the cartel and watch the body crumble."

"We take out the top dog, and the next in line will simply slide into place," Ricky said, his focus on his brother rather than Ryker. "You better believe they'll retaliate, too."

"Unless we take out the men around Arturo and those he shares blood with," Sin offered with a shrug as though jetting down to Columbia to wipe out a few dozen people would be a cake walk.

"Then we instigate a war between Arturo and the other cartel battling for ground," Ryker said. "Let them do the dirty work for us."

"Or we do nothing for now and see where the chips fall." Warden crossed his arms, but his gaze flitted to Shaun who still stood at the bar with her back to us, putting frothing beer mugs onto a tray. The worry that flitted over his face settled in my bones as well.

Arturo, alive, promised trouble in our future like a ticking time bomb—for more than one brother's woman. I hadn't claimed Giada, but my head and gut told me she belonged to me same as Shaun did to Warden.

"What do we do?" I asked Vigil, my fists on my thighs, torn from telling them the truth about the Burtonelli I wanted to protect more than my own life.

"Burtonelli have any ties with the mafia?" Vigil asked Warden.

"Nothing above ground. Nothing he brought up even though we've got an NDR in place, but we know that fucker has attempted to bury other sins from his past."

"Ryker?" our president turned to face him.

Ryker shrugged, his face unreadable. He grew up in Southie, hanging with a handful of the mafia's goons before hooking up with the Vipers twenty years earlier. "Could be. I've been away from the scene for a long fucking time, but I could ask around. See what shit I can dig up."

Vigil nodded. "Stirring up the shit pot between the local mafia family and Arturo would keep him preoccupied for a while at least. Maybe they'll take care of the problem so we can keep our hands clean."

Shaun arrived with our beers and passed them out before settling on Warden's knee, facing the table. "Looking for a way to do away with Arturo?"

Christ knew she held no love for the fucker. Because of him, her mother had died. Her father met his end. He'd also threatened to make her his sex slave when he'd held her captive.

"Club business," Vigil muttered and glared at Warden with a silent order to keep his old lady out of it.

Shaun snorted, her arms crossing. "I just found out I'm rich as fuck. I have my father's contacts—hit men out the ass. Say the word, and I'll make it happen."

Ryker actually fucking chuckled in the silence that rushed in. "Wildcat."

Warden patted her thigh. "I don't want that kind of shit on your conscious, sweetheart."

Vigil stared at her, as did Ricky, both quiet, their

minds probably working hard as fuck while they ignored the beers in front of them.

Ryker tipped his back and slugged his beer down, slamming the empty glass onto the table when he finished. "I say let the little girl spend her daddy's money to take out the fucker that ended him. Fucking justice if you ask me."

"I'm not an officer, but I gotta agree with Ryker," Sin threw in his two cents, the bloodthirsty prick.

I glanced at Shaun.

She held Vigil's stare, ignoring Warden's caress on her thigh. "Have you ever seen those Borne movies?"

Vigil nodded.

"Dad made no secret he had a man or two he could pay to take out anyone who thought to fuck with his family. Bragged about it after we watched the first movie together. Why the hell he didn't go that route rather than attempt to take Arturo out himself, I don't know."

"It was personal," Warden mumbled, wrapping his arms around her waist and pulling him back against his chest. "Felt it was his duty."

She huffed. "Stupid jackass." Her voice broke. "I might not be a patched member or officer of the Vipers," she whispered, "but you guys are the only

LYNN BURKE

family I have. If you want Arturo gone, I'll dig through my dad's contacts and find a way to make it happen."

Vigil glanced at Ricky. They both turned toward Ryker without a word, needing his vote as an officer.

"Fuck yes," he said, his arms crossing once more.

Our treasurer, Devil, was on his way home, so all three turned toward Warden next as our Enforcer.

His beard twitched again before he rested his chin on Shaun's shoulder. "You sure about this, Shaun?"

She swallowed and covered his hands with hers before nodding. "Yes."

"Again," Ricky said, sitting back, "taking out the head doesn't do away with the cartel."

"It does away with that asshole," Ryker muttered.

"If Devil is half as good as Warden says he is in sending out encrypted messages," Shaun said, "then no one will be able to trace the hit back to me—or the Vipers."

"I don't like it." Warden's declaration didn't get a single nod or muttered agreement from our brothers.

Vigil's lip curled for a split second, revealing his disgust over the entire situation, though. He scratched his chest while beckoning over one of the

88

club whores with his other hand. "It's been a long, fucking day," he told us although his focus stayed on the woman approaching. "I'm going to drain my balls down a willing throat and pass the fuck out. We'll have a meeting and come to a decision before New Year's."

"Thanks for that visual," Shaun muttered and pursed her lips.

Ryker chuckled again.

Vigil had laid down the law—even though New Year's Eve had been the "or else" date for Burtonelli to drop his bid for the Senate seat. Knowing voicing that thought wouldn't do a goddamn thing, I told Warden about the system Devil and I had set up earlier in the afternoon.

Ten minutes later, our beers drained, I followed Warden and Shaun out into the cold. "You okay, Stone?" he asked, and I shrugged.

"Fucking beat, but I've got next watch."

He opened the passenger door to his truck for Shaun and shut her in a few seconds later.

I still stood hunched in the cold, scanning the club's parking lot and the chain link fence beyond.

"What's your gut tell you about the Burtonelli case?" he asked.

"That Arturo means business. Burtonelli doesn't

step down from the race by New Year's Eve, and he'll make good on his threat."

"I don't like that judge fucker, but he paid us to protect his ass. Stay vigilant. Focused. I'll probably bring Sin on board once he's released from PT. Hell, if you feel you need me to help out, I don't have anything lined up besides installing three security systems with Devil the middle of January."

I nodded. "Might need you for a party the Burtonellis' planned for New Year's Eve. Having a few more on detail that night sure as fuck won't hurt."

"Let me know, brother." Warden clasped my shoulder and rounded the front of his truck.

Shaun gave me a little wave through the passenger window, and I turned on my heel, my stomach in a knot over the fact I had to head back to hell—and the angel who'd been forced to live there.

8

GIADA

Living under Father's roof again sucked donkey balls. I had to drop a photo shoot two days in because he didn't want us going anywhere. A lovely argument took place over the breakfast table, and I silently thanked God Logan hadn't been around to witness it.

I knew I needed to play nice, attempt to keep the peace, but the thought of living that way for eleven months—and my new insatiable need to plaster myself to Logan's body and not being able to, kept me on a razor's edge of pissiness. Add in PMS, and I was the bitch from hell.

Father eventually smashed his palm onto the breakfast table with a hollered "Enough!" snapping my jaw shut. "If you value your life and those of your family, you'll learn to keep your mouth shut, Giada! This is your life for the foreseeable future. Don't fuck it up!"

"Nicolo," Mother murmured, reaching to touch his forearm with her fingertips. "Please, dear. You'll never get that seat in the Senate if you give yourself a heart attack."

"It'll be *her* doing if my heart decides it's exhausted."

I bit my tongue to keep from blurting out shit about his eating habits, never mind his love of cigars and cognac.

"I can imagine it's quite stifling—for all the children," Mother continued as though she hadn't heard him. "Cristian will have to go to school and Marisa to the office with personal bodyguards. I think it's only fair that Giada be allowed the same."

Father huffed and tossed his napkin onto the table. "If she needed to attend college or had a real job, I would agree."

My jaw clenched, but I picked up my coffee and sipped. There was no need to revisit the topic of my job and what he thought of it—he'd made his opinion clear as hell.

"Before you lock yourself away in your office for

the day," Mother said, "we should discuss the final plans for the New Year's Eve party."

Yet another reason to grit my teeth.

Every year, my parents threw a party on December 31st, one they required their three children to attend. While they boozed it up with their high and mighty so-called friends, we'd been forced to endure a boring as hell evening. At least once Marisa and I reached drinking age, we'd been allowed a glass of champagne.

Father didn't trust us—me, more like it—to not make a fool of myself in front of his colleagues, but I'd brought that on myself. God forbid a finally legal girl have fun, get drunk, and dance on the tables out of need to liven the party up a bit.

"What's there to discuss?" Father stood, brushing aside Mother's hand. "I thought you said everything was planned."

"Well, it is." Mother's smile wobbled as she clasped her hands in her lap. "But I thought perhaps we might do somethings a bit different."

"Such as?" he asked, brow raised as he peered down at her as though lording his position as head of household.

"Well." Mother licked her lower lip and glanced at Cristian then Marisa. "Cristian has brought it to my attention that the Leonards are hosting a party of their own for the senior class—dry, of course."

"And Peter asked me to dinner with his family," Marisa added before Father could snap out a no.

His focus jerked toward my sister with a calculated glint in his eye. Peter Reynolds was one of Boston's richest men. Too old for my sister as far as I was concerned, a widow with three grown children close to Marisa's age, but it was her life. Father had been after his support—monetarily—for months from what I'd heard, so I wasn't surprised when he finally nodded.

"Fine, but a guard goes with you."

"And me?" Cristian asked, not bothering to hide the pleading in his tone.

"A guard stays with you at the Leonards and will bring you home first thing in the morning."

Cristian's face broke into a wide grin, and he nodded. "Thank you, Father."

Marisa murmured her thanks as well.

Hope sprang to life in my mind, and I dared to open my mouth. "Janice Rushing sent me an invite to her party."

Father glared at me at the mention of the congressman's daughter. "The society you've made company with is more interested in their looks and social status than I find tolerable."

Janice wasn't a close friend, but she'd made a name for herself as the co-founder and editor in chief of one of the biggest fashion magazines in the world—lucky bitch even had the backing of both her parents when she'd decided to pursue a career outside politics. She also had cash out the ass and sway with her bigwig contacts in the fashion industry as well as the media—online and in paper.

"She's still undecided on her campaign contribution her father suggested..." I offered Father a wink even though minutes earlier he'd been calling me all sorts of lovely names.

He paused, definitely to consider the thought of my actually being an asset for a change.

"Would you at least trust me to put in some good words here and there—remind her of your stances, what you're running on?" I pushed before he shot me down.

Father's lips pursed and he huffed through his nose. "Ever the manipulative one, Giada. Yes, I do trust you to get that job done at least." He turned away, and my smirk turned into a true grin.

Yes!

"Fail to get me the backing of those in her pocket,

though," Father said without looking over his shoulder as he strode away, "and you'll be *confined* to this house until Election Day."

And just like that, my excitement dissolved.

I held zero sway with Janice. She'd probably only invited me because my agent, a good friend of hers, had managed to snag me a tiny image in the Christmas edition of her magazine.

Maybe I'd get lucky, same as with the invite, but I truly doubted it.

At least, I'd be able to escape the house for a few hours and party it up.

Father disappeared, but poked his head back into the dining room before I could push back my chair.

"Our house guards can shadow Cristian and Marisa, and Mr. Stone goes with you," Father said, pointing at me. "As head of our security, I know he'll keep you in line."

I nodded, biting on my lip to keep it from tilting upward.

"Shouldn't he remain here?" Mother asked, her tone worried. "With the number of people we're having—"

"I'll have Mr. Stone bring on a few more Tellier men for the party. He is focused on his task more than the rest of our security. He's the only one I trust to keep *her* out of trouble."

Father disappeared, his word law, and I caught Cristian's eye as he chuckled.

If Father only knew how much trouble—the good kind—I'd gotten into with one Mr. Stone.

———

"You've been avoiding me."

Logan kept his focus on the road ahead of the chauffer driving us.

It'd been three days since Father agreed the Burtonelli children might party it up outside the traditional New Year's Eve bash, and I'd only seen Logan in passing.

Too chicken shit to visit his room late at night, I'd opted to stay hunkered down in my own when I knew he slept at our house. It had been six days since I'd had his hands and mouth on me, his cock so far up my pussy I couldn't remember my name.

"Logan?" I pressed when he didn't respond.

He leaned forward and put the up the privacy window separating us from the hired driver.

Tingles that had sprung to life earlier when he'd held my hand to help me in the car returned in full force, and I squeezed my thighs together to ease the ache, the longing to be filled.

"I told you I'm not as strong as you," he said, sitting back once more, but making no move to reach for me.

"So it's not that you got a sample and decided you had enough?"

Heat flared to life in his eyes, pulsing my clit. "Never."

I smiled, dimples and all, and he groaned.

"You're killing me, Giada."

As much as I wanted to say, "fuck the party, let's drive around all night long and fuck ourselves silly in the back of the limo", I had a job to do for my father.

"My lipstick won't smear," I said, my voice low as I subtly shifted closer.

He stared at my red lips. "The way I want to taste you right now, your pretty little hair-do and that sequin dress wouldn't survive."

I gulped, fire damn near consuming every inch of my skin as a hot flash swept over me.

"Tempting," I whispered.

His gaze smoldered as it lifted to my eyes.

Silence surrounded us, and I wondered if he could hear the pounding of my heart.

The car slowed, and I cursed, glancing out the window beyond Logan.

We'd arrived, but sat three cars back from the hotel's awning. I returned my focus to Logan's face to find his jaw clenched, his nostril's flared. Giddiness lit through the lust holding me hostage, and I giggled.

"We stay for an hour then take a *very* long drive around the city."

"And if asked, the limo driver tells him where we spent half the night?" Logan shook his head. "I don't think so."

My joy faded as the car moved forward one space. Another idea lit. "We could always get a room here at the hotel..."

One of Logan's eyebrows arched.

"We sneak away from the party a bit early—fuck all night long—" I grasped the hard ridge along his left thigh "—and return home at the time Father expects me, him none the wiser."

"Little vixen. You'll be the death of me."

My smile returned as he groaned, his eyes damn near rolling back into his head as he clasped a hand over mine, stilling me from working his cock.

"So what do you say?" I whispered and leaned closer to breathe over his parted lips.

"Yes."

The car stopped, and I sat back, retrieving my small handbag, my hands shaking and panties a soaked mess.

Logan muttered a few curses under his breath while adjusting himself, and I snickered. I wouldn't be the death of him, but I sure as hell planned on torturing him until we could slip away from Janice's party.

He exited the limo first, and I accepted his offer of help, moving my grip to his elbow once out of the car. Rather than question my hold on him, or even look at me for that matter, he scanned the immediate area, his face an unreadable mask.

Energy hummed between us, raising the hairs on my arm as we moved through the door held open by one of the hotel's employees.

I tugged him toward the front desk on the right.

The hotel manager claimed to be booked, but I knew they kept rooms available for emergency. Not above name dropping, I used my father without his knowing—not for the first time.

Key card tucked away in my purse, I once more took Logan's arm and strode toward the hotel's ball room as though I owned the damn place.

Freedom for the night. Freedom to drink more

than a single glass of champagne if I wished, freedom to spread my legs and willingly give—and take—from the man who had burrowed into my brain, my dreams.

Logan Stone might not be good enough for me in others' eyes, but I refused to deny the chemistry between us. Rather, I planned on acting on said connection until sated.

If such a thing was even possible.

But first, I had to get Janice on board with my father's campaign—or at least try, otherwise my life the following eleven months would suck major ass.

9

STONE

New Year's Eve—and Burtonelli didn't have any intention of dropping out of the race like he'd been told to do. While the threat lay over his head personally, I'd been forced to babysit Giada rather than stay at the Burtonelli mansion to protect his ass.

I didn't like it. Not one fucking bit. Keeping the family together proved easier to watch over, *but* if shots went off, or a bomb managed to somehow get planted in the Burtonelli house, at least the children would be safe.

I'd called in Warden and Sin to help cover the party with Greed and the other house guard, knowing full well I put them in possible harm's way. My brothers knew how to contact me in the event of an emergency, and my spidey-sense buzzed under my skin, not allowing me a moment's rest.

Once again, I found myself in a room full of individuals I would never consider my people. Still clutching my arm, Giada all but dragged me toward the middle of the room without greeting a single soul on the way.

I had no doubt who Janice was—the women held the bearing of a queen, the mass of beings in the room her underlings. Tall, beautiful, and regal from her satiny white-blonde hair to her black gown's hem, she screamed affluent. Money. Prestige and power.

At least in the fashion industry.

We stood in line to greet the night's hostess, and I continued to take stock of those in attendance. Unlike the Christmas campaigning party a few days earlier, my black suit, I'd been told, wouldn't be good enough. I'd been outfitted with a tux, compliments of the gorgeous woman hanging on my arm.

The collar and damn bowtie choked. The shoes pinched.

But at least by sight, I fit into Giada's world. Her father had even agreed to the use of a rented limo for the night who would wait nearby to retrieve us once the party ended. To the unknowing eye, I belonged in the back of that limo and in that ballroom full of affluent people, same as her.

Giada had already rented a room, so I had every intention of enjoying the hell out of her and her body, but I knew I had no chance at a future with her. I didn't belong in her world—never would.

That became more apparent as I continued to examine the crowd. I recognized a dozen faces, a few of the younger ones who'd been in attendance at the Christmas party. I noted, too, more than one face from the big screen, and the previous year's Golden Globe winner for best actress.

Or was that an Oscar?

Not that I cared.

Giada finally released her hold on me to air kiss both of Janice's cheeks. They exchanged the usual bullshit compliments that were probably expected before Giada turned toward me.

"This is Logan Stone, my plus one."

I dipped my head in greeting and took her outstretched hand.

She offered more of a grip than I'd expected, her gaze flitting down over me. "Well aren't you a tasty morsel. Wherever did Giada find you?"

I glanced at Giada, not sure what she wanted to reveal about her family's personal business.

"He's my newest conquest," she said with a laugh and wink. "Don't get any ideas, though—and please don't take it personal if we disappear long before the midnight hour. I haven't come close to getting my fill of this man."

"You poor soul." Janice laughed at me and turned back toward Giada, completely dismissing my presence.

I kept my face passive.

A conquest.

Obviously, Giada must be known for such things for my plus one status to be brushed aside so easily by our hostess. My stomach clenched as Giada moved closer to Janice to speak quietly.

I'd expected to be asked what I did for a living, how I fit into their snobbish world. I even half expected Giada to lie about who I was for the sake of her father's race—and I'd been prepared to not judge her for it, either.

She might not have had her fill of *her conquest*—but she'd gotten everything she would from me.

My guts in a fucking knot, I closed myself off and focused on the job at hand. Being the sentinel I'd been hired to be.

A few minutes of buzzed chatter, and Giada moved away, her hand once more clutching my arm.

She grabbed a glass of champagne off a server's tray and made her way toward the edge of the ballroom, pausing here and there to take time to greet others.

Fake kisses, jealous side glances down over her perfect body from her friends' dates—female and males alike. I dipped my head in greeting, but kept my mouth shut, ignoring the jealous and lustful looks from those obsessed with beautiful people or masculinity that threatened their fragile self-confidence.

Twice while making our way toward a dark corner, Giada introduced me as her latest conquest with a small laugh and wink.

Rather than feel embarrassed, my pissiness heightened until I couldn't help but clench my jaw.

"Can you believe this guest list?" Giada asked, her eyes sparkling and smile blindingly bright as we finally stood against the wall. She drank down half her bubbly before pressing her curves against my side. "I don't think my agent has arrived yet, but there are three photographers here that I've been *dying* to work with."

Unmoved, I continued to watch the sea of bodies sucking down alcohol when not stretching their mouths in fake-ass grins.

Giada chatted excitedly for a few minutes,

sharing gossip about this person and that, and I didn't even bother feigning interest.

"Logan."

"Yeah?" I didn't look down at her.

She pinched my arm. "Hey."

I turned toward her, and her smile faded as she peered up at me.

"You shut down on me."

"Why do you care if I'm nothing more than your latest boy toy?"

A flicker of a frown—and she laughed. "Oh my God, Logan, you can't possibly think I meant that about you being a conquest."

"And why would I think anything different when your snobbish friend over there acted as though that fact wasn't anything new under the sun, that I didn't deserve another minute of her time?"

Giada's smile faded, and I read the regret in her eyes. "I told her that to keep her from asking too many questions. I didn't want you to be embarrassed."

"You mean *you* didn't want to be embarrassed if everyone here learned the truth about who your *plus one* is—a hard-working blue collar who has no business brushing shoulders with your society."

She snorted, her brow furrowing. "As if I give a shit what you do for a living."

"Admit it, Giada. I'm a man beneath your station, and having me in your life as anything resembling relationship status would be a hindrance to what you have planned for your future."

The crossing of her arms pushed her tits up high and drew my focus. I snapped it up to her face quick as fuck, though, my insides a fucking mess.

"You don't know the first thing about my dreams, Logan Stone. Don't pretend to know me after one hot as fuck romp in my shower." Chin lifted, she peered up at me, eyes flashing green fire.

My cock twitched, and I scowled. Damn woman.

"Got nothing to say?" she asked, arching high one of her perfectly groomed eyebrows.

A muscle jumped in my jaw as I clenched my teeth, forcing my focus off her face to the crowd around us. Perhaps she told the truth—or perhaps she attempted to manipulate me into giving her my cock she hadn't yet "gotten her fill of".

Even if she told the truth, I didn't belong in her world. Why torture myself by fucking her again knowing nothing could come of it?

A good damn memory to jerk off to, I told myself,

but I wasn't an asshole like those MC romance heroes she'd said she read about.

"Giada!"

I snapped my head around to find a tiny guy approaching—premature white hair with blue tips stuck straight up from his scalp like he'd licked a goddamn light socket. Eyes too blue to be real twinkled as he grinned a toothy, blinding white smile.

"Fab." I noted the joy in Giada's voice and stepped back as they hugged hard like long-lost friends.

Fab? What the hell kind of name is that?

"You look ravishing, darling," Fab said, finally easing off a bit to air kiss both of her cheeks.

"Same!" Giada held him at arm's length and quickly took in his ridiculous tux. Brighter and just as yellow as a golden sun, sequins along the lapels, skinny pants, and four-inch heeled boots—

"This is my friend Logan," Giada said, gesturing at me.

At least she hadn't called me her conquest.

I nodded and stuck out my hand.

One of Fab's perfectly groomed eyebrows arched and he whistled through his teeth while checking me out from head to toe and back up again. "Girl ... where did you *find* this man?" He laughed and took my hand, not waiting for Giada to answer. "A pleasure to meet you, Logan."

"Same." I snipped the word, waiting for him to release his grip on my hand.

"You don't happen to be in need of an agent, are you, Logan?"

Agent—must be Giada's, and he wants me to model?

I bit back my snort. "No, but you're Giada's?"

"Lucky me," he purred. Fab glanced between Giada and me a few times before finally letting go of my hand. "Mmm hmm," he hummed with a grin.

"So those three photographers I've been dying to work with that keep turning you down over the phone?" Giada said, head swiveling to scan the crowd. "They're here—and you need to work your magic, face to face. Don't take no for an answer."

Fab giggled—fucking giggled, and I found my lips twitching. *Fab for fabulous,* I wondered? Flamboyant as hell, he was a confident, cocky fucker that was for sure. Nothing better than meeting someone who knew who they were and owned it.

I realized he was the first real person I'd met that night—even if he did air kiss Giada.

"Drink another champagne and hang here with Logan..." Fab checked me out again, winking when his gaze finally rested on my face. "It's time to work some Fab magic."

He sashayed away, and Giada laughed.

"Quite the character," I mumbled, still smiling.

"He's the *best*." Giada took a huge breath, lifting her gorgeous tits, and let it out in a rush. "So. Back to what we were talking about."

My smile faded, and I closed myself back down, taking another scan of the ball room.

"Logan."

"Yeah." I didn't look at her.

"*Logan*."

I lifted an eyebrow and met her steady gaze.

"How long are you going to stay closed off to me because of this misunderstanding?"

"Closed off?"

She frowned and crossed her arms, her empty champagne glass' stem between two fingers sticking out by her elbow. "Yes, closed off as in shutting me down—out. My first taste of freedom in six days, and you're totally killing it—and not in a good way. I told you the truth."

"I believe you, but this can't happen, Giada. It never *should* have happened."

"Stubborn ass," she grumbled. "I'll change your mind."

"No, you won't."

"I did before. I will again."

We glared at one another for a few seconds, and I had to tear my focus off her face—her fiery eyes and plump, red as hades lips to check out our surroundings again.

"Coward," she said with a sniff.

I jerked my focus back to her face. "I'm doing my fucking job, Giada. Keeping you safe like I've been hired to do."

She sniffed again while holding my stare. "It was Father's life that was threatened, not mine."

"Not directly, but if someone wants to hurt your father, who would they target?"

"Oh, please," she said with a sarcastic laugh. "My father could give two shits about me other than negative press from an untimely death. If they—whoever the hell they are—want to ruin Father, they need to put a bullet through Marisa or Cristian's brain. That would kill him more than losing Mother, even."

I searched her eyes for any trace she hoped the oldest golden child she'd been compared to her whole life would meet their end in such a way. Coming up empty, I mentally stepped back and inhaled slowly, forcing my shoulders to relax.

My cell buzzed in my coat's pocket, and I fished it out, a shot of adrenaline ripping through me at the name on the screen.

"What's up, Warden?" I asked, thoroughly expecting to hear an attempt had been made on the judge's life.

"Call just came in—"

His tone said it all, and I steeled the muscles in my face to keep from revealing the bad news I was about to hear.

"Car accident."

"Who?" I asked, knowing it was one of two.

"Cristian."

Fuck. I peered down at Giada, fighting to remain stoic. "Outcome?"

"Not good." He cursed. "Not good at all."

"We're on our way." I hit end, but kept hold of my cell.

"Logan, what's going on?" Giada asked, her voice small.

Guess I hadn't hid shit from her.

I texted the limo driver rather than answer Giada, telling him to get his ass back to the hotel's entrance to pick us up earlier than planned.

"We have to leave."

Giada stared at me as I shoved my cell back in

my pocket, concern etching her face. *"What's going on?*

"I'll tell you in the car." I grabbed her hand, and she followed willingly.

Fab happened to be in our path for the ballroom doors, and the second he focused on my face, his smile dissolved and he glanced down at Giada. I kept my lips in a thin line, scanning the others around us, my stride not hesitating from getting Giada the hell out of there.

The accident could have been just that—an accident, but I wasn't taking any chances with her life.

"Giada?" Fab asked, scurrying to her side as I pulled her along behind me.

"I gotta go," she told him. "I-I'll catch up with you later, okay? Just work your magic."

I didn't give them time for air kisses or further goodbyes.

The lobby sat mostly empty, and the chatter and music from the party muted as the doors swung shut behind us.

Giada's cell rang as her heels clicked on the marble floor beside me. She opened her purse and glanced at the caller.

"Don't answer that," I said, my voice hard as we stopped a few feet from the doors leading outside.

"But it's my father." She lifted her focus to my face.

"Please," I begged, allowing my stone façade to ease up a bit.

"Logan?" she whispered, her eyes welling.

I pulled her into my arms, effectively keeping her from answering the call that I knew would wreck her.

She clung to me, shaking, being a good girl and not answering when her phone rang twice more while we waited for the limo.

"Turn it off," I whispered.

Giada obeyed without hesitation and returned to my arms the second she dropped the cell back in her small purse.

Mine cell rang—Burtonelli. I ignored his call as well, and the second the limo pulled up outside the hotel's windows, I released Giada and grasped her hand. "Let's go."

I studied the surrounding area through the windows before exiting, my head swiveling non-fucking stop.

"Take a different route than the one here," I barked at the driver as he opened the limo's back door.

The second the door shut behind us, I raised the

privacy window and turned to find Giada's troubled gaze plastered to my face, her hands clutching her purse on her lap.

"Tell me."

"Cristian."

Tears welled, and she swallowed, her pain knifing through my fucking chest. "No," she managed to squeak.

I pulled her into my arms, but she didn't melt against me. She shrieked, beating against my chest, and I bit my lip as sobbed curses ripped from hers.

10

GIADA

I loved wearing black—usually rocked it—but not the black of grief. Sitting in the front of the church alongside Marisa, I stared at the priest's moving mouth, nothing in my ears but a ringing that hadn't ceased since learning the love of my life had lost his in a car accident.

Numbness had crept in before Logan and I had even returned home, denial or my emotions dying along with my baby brother's, I didn't know. I couldn't find it in myself to care about that either.

I'd stood on the outside, watching mother sob as Marisa held her on the love seat, Father staring out his study's window, a glass of cognac clutched in his shaking hand.

Shared grief should have bonded us together, at

the very least, buried all other hurt for a time, but Cristian's death raised the wall between us higher —thicker.

Father's gaze had met mine the second I'd walked in—the hurt pulling me up short of going to Mother. His eyes had said it all.

He wished it had been me in that car.

At least I'd been numb already. I'd managed to look away without the hurt his disappointment always stabbed into my chest.

Three days had passed, and the silence in the house had only been broken by Father's outbursts at everyone who crossed his path. Rather than grieve, he ranted about the stories in the paper, his numbers falling in the polls because he'd bowed out of a debate and two visits to areas he needed to win over in the two days following Cristian's death.

My hatred of the bastard doubled, and while I no longer had my baby brother to keep me from fleeing the house, the family, I couldn't fathom ruining my mother by the loss of a second child in so short a time. She hadn't left her bed in those three days, and I'd only managed to sit with her for five minutes a day before my numbness threatened to ease up.

I sat in my room instead, avoiding everyone, burrowed in a cocoon of escapism with my e-reader.

Thankfully, I managed to lose myself a few times in the stories, but the second I turned off the screen, Cristian's face came to mind, and I couldn't sleep.

Dark circles hung beneath my eyes, and I couldn't find it in myself to care.

I dressed for his funeral with the same amount of giving a fuck, twisting my hair into a knot, going makeup-less. The family had driven in the limo in complete silence.

I'd caught sight of Logan a few times during those days, but couldn't even be bothered to meet his gaze or answer when he asked how I was doing. Twice, he squeezed my hand, and I clenched my teeth to keep from breaking wide open.

Thankfully, he hadn't driven in the limo with the family to the funeral, but I felt his gaze on my back as the priest droned on. I'd heard Logan had insisted on a quiet, private affair rather than a full-on funeral, but Father needed to be seen grieving. Not the type of exposure he'd said he wanted—but losing his only son and being seen in his grief would only help him gain those numbers back he'd lost.

I wondered if he was bastard enough to be thankful for the exposure, a part of him in some sick way happy his only son had died.

My jaw ached from clenching my teeth, my feet

itched to move, to take off far away from the pain I squashed deep inside me. The funeral finally ended, thank fucking hell.

Close to a dozen Vicious Vipers showed up for the final goodbyes at the cemetery, their black leather vests clearly stating what club they rode with. Although they hadn't known Cristian, hadn't been hired by Father to watch over the rest of us, they spread out around the small group by Cristian's grave, focused on our surroundings rather than the casket.

Standing by the gaping black hole, I stared dried eye. Tightness rose to my throat, but I refused to be moved even when placing a single rose atop the box his body would rot inside.

One long as hell ride to the country club—a celebration of Cristian's life—a chance for me to drink a few while Father was preoccupied chatting with people as though truly thankful they attended. The fucker just wanted their support.

The Vipers hadn't been invited, and I noted only a few of our family's friends—most eating and drinking on my father's dime, had been invited for political gain, of that I had no doubt. Even Cristian's best friends from school and their parents hadn't been included in the so-called celebration. Neither had his beard of a girlfriend, the poor girl.

Cristian's guard had wrapped the car around a tree while driving him to his friend's house that night. Head trauma had taken my brother along with his guard, and I hoped it had been quick enough he hadn't felt a goddamn thing.

The thought of his suffering even for more than a split second hurt too much to handle. At least the wine helped keep my numbness in place while having to listen and graciously accept condolences every few minutes.

We finally arrived home in early evening, and I escaped without a word to my room, stripped down, and sat in the tub. Steam rose, heat soaking into my limbs that had frozen through while at the grave site and hadn't thawed at the country club.

Silence rang in my ears, and I closed my eyes. The tightness once more rose to choke me, and I finally allowed myself to let go.

———

I've heard it said that time heals all wounds, but the hurt from having your favorite person in the whole world ripped from your life hangs on with stubborn bitchiness even though the hours slide by.

Only two weeks had passed, two long as fuck weeks where the raw grief remained, and neither Marisa nor I were allowed to leave the house. She, at least, was able to work remotely, while my career suffered. Not that I wanted to smile or give a camera smoldering looks while photographers gushed about how gorgeous I was.

I spoke with Fab a few times, but even the good news of his getting me two of those three longed-for photo shoots for later in the spring couldn't entice me to find joy in life. At least I no longer sobbed myself to sleep every night.

The numbness had returned in full force, and I felt like a damn zombie, going through the motions of eating sawdust-like food and only showering after realizing my armpits stank to high hell.

My bed became my newest best friend, same as Mother.

Drawn and shaky, she sat at the table three times a day at Father's command, but only managed to push her food around on her plate with a fork. She lost weight, her cheeks sunken, so I forced myself to eat at least a little to keep from wasting away like she appeared to be doing.

I saw Cristian's smiling face in my dreams, his twinkly eyes—I saw his head smash against the car's window—and I'd wake, my heart in my throat.

After almost fourteen days of the same fucking dream waking me every damn night, I lay in bed, shivering, the images in my head on replay—and I couldn't make them stop.

I considered reading, but hadn't been able to focus on words the previous couple of days. Needing distraction, needing to just *move*, I crawled out of bed, wrapped myself in my robe, and crept out into the hallway thinking I could hide away in the media room and watch a movie.

Silence met my ears, and I turned toward the stairs.

Logan stood at the foot, in jeans and a long-sleeve t-shirt.

The new cameras ... of course he'd seen me leave my room if he'd been on watch.

For the first time in over two weeks, I met his gaze, the compassion without an ounce of pity in his eyes sweeping the numbness from my mind and heart. Tears slid down my cheeks, and I rushed to meet him, throwing myself in his arms.

"So sorry, baby."

I couldn't speak, but clung to his hard body, his

strength, as silent tears fell. Once I stopped crying, he led me into the closet being used as a security room, sat on the office chair in front of a half dozen computer screens, and pulled me onto his lap.

Snuggling in with a sigh, I breathed in his scent that I'd forgotten in my grief. Warmth encased me, a sense of peace seeming to drape over me as though his arms shielded me from the pain.

We sat in silence for a time, his fingertips gently rubbing my back, his lips sometimes brushing over the top of my hair. I realized I hadn't washed my hair for at least three days—and I actually cared.

"Sorry," I whispered as his heart thumped against my ear.

"You don't have to apologize, Giada."

"My hair needs washed—I need to shower. I stink."

"I don't care."

Silence fell again, and I sighed, my eyes closing as I focused on the feel of his hard chest and arms cradling me. A twinge of interest woke between my thighs, easing *that* numbness I'd been experiencing since Cristian's death.

Exhaling slowly, I decided to allow myself emotion. Allowed my body to react, respond in whatever the hell way it wanted—I needed to live since Cristian couldn't.

"Unable to sleep?" Logan's hot breath caressed my forehead before I could make a move.

"Nightmares." The truth spilled unintended and snapped all thoughts of arousal from my body.

"Want to talk about them?"

I kept my eyes wide open so I wouldn't be faced with the horror again. "I see Cristian's head splatter against the car's window."

"Shit," Logan muttered, squeezing me tighter. "I'm so fucking sorry."

"I just hope he didn't suffer."

"Me, too." Logan kissed my forehead again, and I realized I'd tensed up. A slow, steady inhale and exhale, counting to eight, and I melted against his chest once more, taking comfort in his gentle hold.

Totally relaxed for the first time since I could remember, I decided to sleep right where I was and gave over to the darkness where no pain existed.

11

STONE

"It was Arturo."

Devil's declaration jerked my head up from my cell, and I met his gaze across the table. Vigil and Ryker sat with us at the club, having a few drinks to unwind from the week, and both men tensed as I did at the mention of that fucker's name.

"Say again?" I asked.

Devil looked up from the laptop that always sat in front of him even when the club rocked around us. "He's the one responsible for the Burtonelli kid's supposed accident."

"Fuck." I scrubbed a hand down over my face. "You're sure?"

"As fuck. Got the damn emails to prove it."

"Any news on his whereabouts?" Vigil asked

while I considered the non-accident that had stolen two lives—and what Burtonelli's reaction might be to that news.

"Arturo disappeared off the goddamn map," Devil muttered, scowling. Our tech wiz hadn't been able to track him down through any of his usual sneaky-ass means.

Arturo had left his estate in Columbia, his plane enroute to Boston, but he'd never arrived. While I'd hoped his aircraft had gone down in the gulf, we hadn't heard news of any going down, nor had Devil been able to learn where Arturo's plane had landed.

He could be anywhere—and with no knowledge of his whereabouts, the hitman Devil had helped Shaun get in touch with sat on his hands awaiting orders.

"We gotta tell Burtonelli the truth," Devil said, glancing up at me. "About the origin of the threats and his son's non-accidental death."

I turned toward Vigil, needing his input even though the Vipers weren't directly involved with Tellier Security. I'd been pleased as hell, though, that a few of my brothers had attended the burial where the family had been out in the open, easy pickings.

"Fucker will want Arturo's head, that's for damn

sure," Ryker added his thoughts as Vigil seemed to consider.

"We give Burtonelli the info," Vigil finally said, "and we make him a deal—we do away with the threat once and for all, and he keeps his nose out of our business when he takes office."

"Would be better if the fucker owed us one in return," Ryker suggested, flagging the pledge behind the bar and holding up four fingers for another round. "Something to keep in our back pocket for the future."

"And if he doesn't get elected?"

"How about we *help* him get elected?" Vigil said, sitting back, a gleam in his eye. "Win-win."

I nodded—and so did Devil. Ryker held Vigil's gaze for a few seconds. "Ricky will be on board."

Vigil nodded. His brother, our VP, had gotten clean after a few years living in hell. He'd paid a massive price for his poor decisions in more ways than one. A campaign to rid New England of the opioid epidemic had been his desire since sobering up.

"Want me to call Warden?" I asked, but Vigil shook his head.

"We all know where his thoughts on Arturo lie." Vigil slapped his palms on the table, startling the approaching pledge with his tray of beers, but the kid kept his balance, not spilling a drop.

"Stone, can you get us a meeting with his hind-ass?" Vigil asked once the pledge disappeared again.

"Burtonelli eats breakfast like clockwork every day at seven. Show up at seven-fifteen, and he'll have no choice," I said. "Otherwise, you might get brushed off."

"Tomorrow," Vigil said, nodding. "I'll let Ricky and Warden know. We'll meet here at six-thirty and drive down together."

———

Even though I wasn't one of the Viper officers, I stood at the back of Burtonelli's home office along with Ryker and Warden as Vigil told him the news Devil had dug up concerning the origin of the death threats and the non-accident that had ripped his son from the family.

Burtonelli had hated being interrupted while eating breakfast, but I'd insisted quietly in his ear as he sat at the head of the table that he would want to hear what the Vipers' officers had to say.

"You know this how?" Burtonelli asked, his face flushing and eyes hardening into a scowl as he sat behind his desk like a damn wannabe dictator across from Vigil, Devil, and Ricky.

Vigil nodded at Devil who pulled three sheets of paper from his leather case and handed them over to the judge.

Burtonelli read over the information the officers had been informed of the night before. "A second car?" he muttered, glancing up at Devil.

"The original police report was buried in exchange for a mere ten grand."

"And how do you know Arturo ordered my son's car run off the road?"

"See page two."

Burtonelli flipped over to the second paper, his lips thinning. "Fucking hell." He swallowed, the muscles in his jaw flexing repeatedly while reading. "You're sure this email was sent by Arturo?" he asked, his voice the slightest bit shaky.

"We've had our eye on him for months," Devil said with a shrug. "I got myself a nice little collection of love letters from the fucker to various contacts of his. All encrypted, of course, but I figured his ass out."

"The FBI would have done away with him if gaining this sort of information proved this easy,"

Burtonelli argued as though to convince himself Devil lied.

Devil grinned. "FBI doesn't have the skills I do."

Burtonelli's lips thinned again as he scanned the rest of the emails—including the final page where Devil had included the original death threat sent to the judge's email—and the last order to take out the heir since Burtonelli hadn't bowed out of the race by the date he'd been ordered to—New Year's Eve.

"I want his mother fucking blood," the judge spat, his face twisting as he fisted the printout in his trembling hand.

"And we're going to spill it for you," Vigil said.

"At what cost?"

"A favor."

Burtonelli stared him down, waiting.

"I'll let you know when the time comes," Vigil supplied the answer to the judge's unspoken question.

The two men continued to stare at one another, neither shifting.

"I don't like to be indebted," Burtonelli finally said.

"You want him gone. We've got the contacts to make that happen—unless you've got another idea to do away with the head of the cartel, the fucker who's willing to pay over a million to keep you out of the Senate?"

A muscle spasmed in Burtonelli's clean-shaven jaw again. "You could hand this information over to the FBI and allow them to do their job."

"And how long would the legal course of action take?" Vigil crossed his arms. "As you read in that last email Devil intercepted, you've got until February first—less than two weeks to drop out, or else."

The clock on the wall ticked loudly in the stillness as Burtonelli considered.

"What say you, good man?" Vigil pushed, his arms crossing.

Burtonelli ignored him, taking in each man in his office—their cuts, the hard gazes, the promise of violence, the viciousness our club was known for. He finally nodded, probably not wanting to voice his agreement out loud—just in case.

Fuck knew he didn't need any more sins littering his past.

Vigil stood, offering his hand over the desk. "It was good doing business with you, *Senator*."

Burtonelli wasn't as quick to rise, by he shook our president's hand. "A bit premature, but I'll take your vote of confidence."

"It's not confidence, Burtonelli," Vigil told him, their hands still tightly clasped. "It's assurance."

Burtonelli's chin tilted upward as they both stepped back, his gaze narrowing.

"Let's just say the Vipers like the change you're promising to make once elected," Ricky said while rising from his chair beside his brother, speaking up for the first time since arriving. "And we have ways of helping to get you that seat."

The judge peered at Ricky before turning back to Vigil. "Care to share those ways?"

Vigil didn't crack a smile, but Devil did. "I have a ... knack, shall we say, at uncovering unsavory bits of peoples' pasts they've tried to bury. The man running against you..."

I half expected Burtonelli to wonder over the anonymous extortionist that had fattened the Vipers' pockets over his past indiscretions, but no flicker of suspicion crossed his face. Thank fuck my brothers knew how to keep their own emotions on lockdown.

"Gentlemen." Burtonelli straightened, righting his suit coat. "I think this is the beginning of a long and beneficial friendship."

Vigil dipped his head once in agreement—and the Vipers filed out of the office.

12

GIADA

I settled into a routine, dragging my ass out of bed around ten. Swim in our indoor, heated pool, shower, eat, read, watch TV, nap, eat again... Boring as hell, but the time passed.

Mother began eating again, but I'd yet to see a smile or trace of laughter from anyone in the house.

Cristian had been gone for almost a month, and even though the pain had faded enough I could function and sleep, tears tracked my cheeks daily. I'd offered to help pack up his things and donate them to the needy, but Mother wouldn't hear of facing the truth Cristian wouldn't ever sleep in his bed or wear the clothes in his chest of drawers and closet. It would come eventually, so I didn't push. I just needed something to *do*.

Marisa continued to work out of her old bedroom, but Father wouldn't even allow Fab to visit —or any other of my friends for that matter. I refused to cancel the photo shoots he'd scheduled for me in the hopes that Father would change his mind in the weeks ahead.

The thought of having Logan watch me work in front of a camera lit tingles between my thighs.

He'd been around, but completely shut down and unavailable after holding me that night. I'd woken in my bed the next morning, not remembering having walked back up the stairs and down the hallway or even crawling beneath my blankets.

My need for dick returned, and my vibrator wasn't cutting it.

Logan sat in the security room off the foyer as I lay in bed. Alone. Unsatisfied. Needy. It hadn't taken much to make him cave the first time...

I glanced over at my alarm clock, the blue numbers acting as a nightlight. Father and Mother always retired by ten. That hour had fled by, and I'd heard Marisa shut herself in her room across the hallway at least a half-hour earlier while I'd been reading my favorite author's newest MC novel. The dirty-talking hero and the first sex scene had me reaching for my vibrator.

But I needed more.

Nibbling my lower lip, I slid out of bed, listening at the door with my ear pressed against it.

Logan would know the second I slipped into the hallway. Would he meet me in the foyer again or ignore me, thinking I needed a late-night snack as I'd done twice before in the previous weeks when unable to eat dinner over Father's bitching?

Time to find out.

I turned the knob and eased the door open, slipping into the quiet hallway with a slow exhale. Door once more silently shut behind me, I crept down the hallway to the balcony overlooking the foyer.

No Logan, I noted, my bare feet cold on the wooden treads. The security room/closet's door stood cracked open a good six inches, and I could see Logan's thigh where he sat at the desk. His fingers tapped on his knee as I reached the landing and started his way.

I pushed in the door, and he finally turned to look up at me. "Everything alright?"

"Couldn't sleep."

His gaze narrowed as he studied my face—as though he read the lie on my face.

"Can I curl up on your lap again?"

He let out a heavy exhale, but didn't say no.

I snicked the door shut behind me and sat—straddling him rather than curling like I'd asked, the t-shirt I wore to bed riding high up my thighs.

"Giada," he half-groaned my name, his hands coming to rest inches from my aching core.

I slid closer, my hands grasping at his nape, his short hair tickling my palms. "I need you."

The muscle in his sharp jaw clenched, his blue eyes full of lust—and regret. "We can't do this."

"Sure we can." I licked over his bottom lip, and his fingertips dug into my skin. "Everyone else is sleeping. No one can see us in here," I whispered, our breath hot against each other's mouths.

"Goddamn you, Giada." He took my lips with a bruising kiss, jerking me tight against his swelling cock.

I moaned and ground myself against his length as he owned my mouth. Obliterated everything but need from my head. My skin came alive beneath his touch as he shoved my shirt around my waist, his fingers finding my soaked core smearing all over his jeans.

He shoved two fingers deep inside me, and I gasped into his mouth, biting at his lip.

"More."

A third—and I saw fucking stars as he tangled his hand in my hair and took me deeper with his tongue and lips. My pussy pulsed around his thrusting fingers—but it wasn't enough.

I wrenched my head back, his hold tingling my scalp—and shooting lust straight to my clit. "I want you inside me, Logan. Now."

He pulled his fingers from my dripping pussy and licked them clean while I fumbled to free his cock. The deep groan rumbling his chest from my taste sent another rush of wetness, readying my pussy for his big cock.

A shift of his hips along with my frantic hands freed him, and he yanked me into his arms—and down onto his jutting length with one thrust.

"Oh, God." I gasped, my gaze ensnared by his.

"Fuck yourself on my dick, Giada."

Yes, fucking, sir.

I lifted and lowered, ground my clit against his pelvis, working the hell out of my thighs and abs, all the while fighting off the tingles in my toes that promised climax.

"You feel so fucking good, baby." He grasped one of my tits and held it up to his mouth while I bounced on him. "Tight." Nibble. "Wet." A deep suck. "Fucking heaven."

My climax hovered, and I closed my eyes, panting and licking my lower lip.

"Come all over my dick. Cream me up good, baby."

Logan reached between us and snagged hold of my clit with two fingers, squeezing—fucking pinching me.

I inhaled to let out a shriek, and he crashed his lips against mine, swallowing my cries as my pussy clamped down on his thrusting length. He groaned into my mouth, every stab of his cock against my cervix drawing out my climax.

Heat erupted deep inside me, his dick pulsing as he grunted.

Breathless, I sagged against his chest, our hearts pounding in time.

Yes. Fucking yes.

A sated, sticky mess, I smiled while coming back down to earth.

Logan exhaled heavily. "Goddamnit, Giada." Regret laced his tone.

"Don't you dare shut down on me," I muttered as he shifted me away from his chest, his cock still thick inside me.

He glanced around me, his brow furrowed—checking the cameras, I realized. "This has to stop."

"No chance in hell," I murmured, still smiling and reaching up to drag my fingernail down his t-shirt tightly enclosed over his hard chest.

Logan grasped my hand and stopped me.

I lifted my focus to his eyes—his beautiful, closed off blue eyes. "Stubborn ass."

"Twice now you've gotten me to let down my guard, and it can't happen again." He peered at me, a muscle in his jaw clenching. "I know you can't stand your father, but if something happens to him on my watch when I'm fucking around with you rather than doing my job, you'll never forgive me."

I opened my mouth to tell him he didn't know just how much I couldn't stand my prick of a father, but he continued.

"Think of your mother. Your sister. They would lose him, too."

My lips pressed tightly together. I hated that he had a point.

Our breaths sounded loud in the small room that smelled of sex and lilacs. The most luscious, head-spinning scent in the world...

My heart clenched as his eyes shut down on me—as he shut me out. "You don't want me."

"I have to protect your father, Giada."

He's choosing Father over me.

I climbed off his lap onto shaky legs, our cum dripping down my thighs. Swallowing against the tightness in my throat, I turned and let myself out, his lack of calling after me telling me all I needed to know.

———

The days passed, and February arrived—along with two other new guards from Tellier Security.

I didn't ask. Didn't care.

When Father insisted the whole family attend his rally in some hoe-bunk town in western Mass, I gritted my teeth. While I hated the idea of being stuck in a car with him for a few hours, I would at least get a change of scenery.

He bitched the entire ride, not that I'd expected otherwise.

At least no guard sat in the back with us to hear his rants, see his childish pouting. Narcistic asshole. Prick.

And, it only got worse when we arrived and he took to the stage.

He milked Cristian's death for all it was worth,

fake ass tears in his eyes and all, working the crowd for their compassion.

My stomach churned, and I'd had enough.

Fuck this, and fuck the family. I'm done.

Father's guards stood around the room, Greed and Drew Tellier himself, aka Warden, behind the podium. I eyed the door to my left where I sat at the end of the aisle. One of the house guards stood ahead of it, facing the stage.

Logan, I knew, stood at the back of the cavernous hall, far enough away I'd be able to sneak off once the crowd got going.

Ten minutes later, Father's voice rose, his fist pumping the air about some bullshit or another, and the crowd surged to its feet and cheered. I slipped out of my chair, eyeing the guard who didn't turn my way. Three quick steps put me in front of the door.

Heart pounding, I eased it shut behind me quietly even though the crowd continued to cheer and chant Father's name. A bunch of sheep led by a liar—typical politician and the fucktwat idiots who couldn't think for themselves—couldn't discern the bullshit face he put on in the hopes of gaining power.

Adrenaline rushed through me as I clutched my coat and purse close, hurrying up the inclined hallway. I expected a guard stood sentry in the lobby—if so, I'd use the excuse of looking for the bathroom.

An exit sign overhead pointed down another hallway to my right, and I hesitated all of two seconds before hurrying that way instead of toward the lobby.

I would need to get an Uber or taxi ... and pray they'd take me all the way back east to my condo where I'd left behind more than enough personal belongings to grab for my flight.

Vegas, I told myself, hurrying toward the door directly ahead of me with the glowing exit sign above.

A hand grasped my arm from behind, and I shrieked.

"Where the hell are you going?"

Logan. Fuck.

I gulped, my heart pounding, suddenly breathless. "Leaving," I managed, my voice shaking.

He scowled. "What do you mean *leaving*?"

"Getting the fuck out of here—away from Father, away from *you*!"

Logan jerked me back the way we'd come.

"Let me go!" I hissed, beating at his arm with my purse.

He shoved in a door—janitor's closet—and did

as I'd asked, slamming the door shut behind him and flicking on a light.

"Don't leave me." His words took the air right out of my damn sails, and I sagged, all fight gone in a flash.

"I-I didn't think you wanted me."

Logan took a step closer, his gaze flooding with so much more than lust. "I don't just want you—I fucking *need* you."

My purse fell to the floor, my coat right along with it, and he closed the short distance between us, yanking me up into his arms, his hungry mouth attacking mine. I met him bruising kiss for bruising kiss, lashing teeth and moans, grasping at his suit coat, his shoulders.

He reached beneath my skirt and ripped my panties off, shoving two fingers inside me before I realized what he'd done.

"God," I groaned, tipping my head back as he nipped at my chin, my jaw.

"This pussy..." He finger fucked me while sucking on my neck, his deep growls and groans enticing wetness out of me as much as his thrusting fingers.

"Gonna come," I gasped as he rubbed deep inside my inner wall.

Holding his gaze as he pulled away to look into my eyes, I panted, waiting for the tingles in my toes to sweep up and over my body, for my climax to own me as his fingers and gaze did. The wet sounds of his fingers fucking into me battled our heightened breaths to fill the silence around us.

My breath caught once—twice—and then my climax took control of my body.

"Giada," he whispered my name like he worshiped at my feet, his fingers drawing every last spasm from my pussy as I whimpered and gasped for breath.

He backed off, quick as fuck, touching the mic on his lapel, his mask slipping back into place as he glanced away. "Come again?"

Someone spoke in his ear, I realized as his face hardened and lips pursed.

Muffled screams sounded outside the closet's door—my heart stopped as our gazes collided.

"Stay here!" Logan barked at me and spun to leave.

"Logan! What's going on?" I shrieked as he yanked open the door.

"Shots fired!" He slammed the door behind him, and I stood trembling. Alone and breathless. My heart in my throat, my mind buzzing, all trace of satiated bliss ripped from my body at his two words.

I huddled in a corner, my fist against my mouth, more worried he ran toward danger than what might have happened to the rest of my family.

13

STONE

People flooded the hallway, and I fought against the crowd, desperate to get to where they'd escaped from.

Distracted ... and look what the fuck happened...

"Where's the shooter?" I shouted at Warden in the small mic on my coat.

"Shots came from the back—where are you?"

Not where the fuck I was supposed to be.

"I'm headed your way." I hugged the wall, shoving and pushing as much as the screaming people rushing past, desperate to get to the podium where Warden had told me they'd gone down when shots fired. "Burtonelli?"

"Senator took one to the shoulder—Marisa to the face."

"Fuck!" He must have called her onto stage after I'd followed Giada out of the hall.

"She's alive," Warden's voice came through the earpiece before I could ask. "Greed's on the phone with 911."

"Shooter down!" Sin hollered, out of breath—he and one of the family guards had been stationed at the back exit.

A stream of people still attempted to get through the side door where Giada had escaped from, but I shoved past, not bothering to help up a young guy I knocked to the floor.

Warden huddled on the podium, gun in hand, face stern as he watched the crowd, his back to the fallen judge and daughter. Mrs. Burtonelli sprawled over Marisa, and her shrieks reached my ears above those of the crowd still jammed in the massive room.

Greed stood off to the side, cell tucked against his ear and talking, his gun also out and at the ready, scanning the crowd. One of the family guards knelt by the judge.

I rushed onto the stage, a quick glance down letting me know Burtonelli would live—his guard pressed a handful of tissues against his bleeding shoulder, his face pale as death even though no other bullet holes appeared to have ripped through his suit.

Marisa lay alongside him, one side of her face a mangled, fucking mess, her mother sobbing over her unmoving form.

"Goddamnit." I knelt beside her, my fingers on her neck. A slow, but steady pulse thumped against my fingertips.

"She's gonna be okay," I told Mrs. Burtonelli while twisting to pull the judge's hankie from his suit coat. "Hold this!" I barked at his wife while pressing it to the side of Marisa's face oozing with blood.

Mrs. Burtonelli continued to sob, her gut wrenching cries twisting my stomach, but I pulled myself away.

"Where's Giada?" Warden asked, his back still toward us as the crowd melted out the exits.

"Safe."

Sirens sounded, and I sprinted up the center aisle, pressing the button on my mic again. "Where are you, Sin?"

"Out front to the left—cops just arrived."

"Fucker still alive?"

"Couldn't take the chance, Stone. Had to put him down."

Lips pursed, I shoved my gun back in its shoulder holster and slammed open the door, stepping into the bright sunshine—and frigid cold. My breath fogged with quick pants as I scanned my surroundings.

At least ten cop cars swarmed the parking lot— cops rushing my way and more toward my right.

"Burtonelli is behind the podium with two security officers," I told the cops as they approached.

They rushed past me with drawn guns—the reason I'd put mine away even though there could have been another shooter.

Sin stepped back from a sprawled form on the ground as the cops approached him. He, too, put his gun away as they neared, shouting at him to do so.

One cop grabbed him by the bum arm, and I caught Sin's wince as he shoved my brother to the ground.

"I'm with the security detail!" Sin hollered but lay still, allowing them to do their job without resistance.

EMTs approached me, bags jostling in their hands.

"Two down behind the podium," I told them, turning to lead the way and raising my voice so they'd hear me. "Judge took a bullet to the shoulder, his daughter to her face. Steady pulse, but she's unconscious."

The cops had swarmed the stage, but at least Warden and Greed hadn't been thrown to the ground like Sin.

Praying like fuck Giada had stayed put—and there wasn't a second shooter—I sprinted back toward the closet I'd left her in.

Death-like silence hovered over the hallway, my feet slamming into the carpet with muffled stomps as I rushed to get back to her. Adrenaline rushed through my blood, thumping heartbeats in my ears.

Please be there. Please be there.

I yanked the door handle and shoved it in —darkness.

"Logan!" Giada's shriek rushed relief through me, and her barreling body nearly tackled me to the ground as I flicked on the light, her hands running all over me, her gaze a frantic caress from the top of my head to my chest and back up before I yanked her against me. "You're alright," she said with a sob against my chest.

I crushed her to me, so fucking relieved she was alright, that my damn throat tightened my breath right the fuck off.

I'd been distracted—and it could have cost

Marisa her life. Arturo might have won that round, but time would tell. Had I been at the hall's back corner where I'd been stationed rather than following after Giada, I might have been able to stop the shooter.

Knowing I'd protected Giada should have eased my guilt.

It didn't, and I fought Pop's whisperings of failure in the back of my head.

14

GIADA

I curled up in the back of the limo, exhaustion hovering. Marisa and Father had been life-flighted to Mass General, along with Mother who'd refused to be left behind.

I'd stuck to Logan's side like a festering cyst in the hours following the shooting while he spoke with the cops and his team.

Even the FBI showed up with a million questions.

No one recognized the shooter who'd taken Sin's bullet between the eyes. No identification on the man left the law in the dark, but since I hung on Logan's side, I heard exactly who had sent the fucker who might have killed my sister.

A cartel leader from Columbia—not the best

enemy for my father to have. At least, that's what Logan had heard rumor of, or so he'd stated.

I wondered, though.

Although Greed also rode with us, the two men didn't converse, and I appreciated the silence.

My cell dinged, and I lifted my head off Logan's shoulder to swipe the screen open.

Mother: **Marisa is still in surgery, but the doctor just came out to tell me that everything is going well. Your father is here in recovery, also doing well. I'm staying the night with him at the hospital, so please let me know when you get home.**

I typed a single letter—**K.**

It's all I had energy for before dropping my cell, exhaling heavily, laying down, and placing my cheek on Logan's hard thigh.

"Giada?" he asked, his voice loud in the stillness of the limo we shared.

"Father's in recovery and Marisa is still in surgery. Doing good, Mother says."

Logan smoothed my hair off my forehead, tucking strands behind my ear. "How are *you* doing?"

I managed a shrug. Exhaustion had rattled my brain, and every inch of me ached, especially my toes from the Jimmy Choos I'd been standing in all damn day. Twice, Logan had tried to get me to eat something, but I'd been too upset to stomach the thought of food.

I'd wanted to escape earlier that morning—had taken steps to do so before Logan had found me. Had I not gone my own way, would I have ended up with a bullet in my body like Marisa's? Father had called his family up on stage, I'd overheard from the non-stop chatter, and I wondered if he'd even been upset I'd disappeared.

The first shot had come as he'd hugged Marisa. She slumped against Father, and the next shot to his shoulder spun them around and to the floor. In the pandemonium, would the shooter have attempted to take me out, too?

Fear of future attempts on my family's life—my life—had my tired feet itching to run even though Logan's presence filled the rest of me with calmness.

I couldn't run—not with Marisa straddling the door between life and death, not with a long recovery if she survived surgery. Mother would be devastated.

"Try to get some sleep," Logan murmured, caressing my shoulder.

"Can't."

"Here," Greed said.

Logan reached forward, his stomach pressing into the back of my head, but I couldn't even open my eyes to see what for.

Glass clinked and liquid poured.

"Giada?" Logan touched a glass to my limp hand, and I roused my eyelids.

Father's cognac he kept in the back of his car.

I propped up on my elbow and swallowed the flowery liquid down, feeling the coolness slide all the way into my stomach. Handing back the empty glass, I snuggled against Logan's thigh once more and shut my eyes.

Logan had kept me from seeing Marisa—thank fuck. Nightmares of Cristian were bad enough. I didn't need real images flashing through my brain. I'd seen Mother, though, pale as a ghost, her makeup streaked down her cheeks and smeared around her eyes. She'd given me one, hard hug upon finding me uninjured, but she'd gone back to Father's side as he ranted and raved at the EMTs and law enforcement, trying unsuccessfully to quiet him.

Logan had gotten an earful about not doing the job he'd been hired to do—and he strode away from those of us still in the hall the second the EMTs wheeled Father away.

Instantly, my body had tensed, my heart seized, and I'd hurried after him.

He hadn't been able to rid himself of me after that. He'd been all business, his face a mask, cold and unfeeling, but I didn't take it personally.

Darkness crept in around the edges of my mind, and I gave over with a sigh.

It seemed seconds later that someone whispered my name, rousing me enough to realize the car no longer moved beneath me.

Home. Finally.

I pushed up from Logan's lap, blinking in the floodlights spilling from the front of my parents' house. Not home. I hadn't thought to ask where Logan would take me, but I shouldn't have been surprised considering his determination to do his job.

Logan opened the door, and cold air blasted me in the face, but I slid toward his outstretched hand, squeezing it tight.

"Shoes," I muttered, my teeth starting to chatter.

"I'll grab them," Greed said from behind me. "Got your coat and purse, too."

Logan swept me up into his arms, and I burrowed in close, his shoes scuffing the pavers leading to the stairs. The door swished open as though someone had opened it for us—probably Father's driver—and I sighed at the warmth of the foyer.

I expected to be set on my feet, but Logan carried me up the stairs to my bedroom.

Greed followed us in, putting my purse on the dresser and shoes beside it. "I'll take first watch," he said quietly, and shut the door behind him.

Logan sat me on the edge of the bed, and I stared bleary-eyed as he rummaged through the dresser.

"T-shirt," I muttered, and he grabbed one out of the next drawer.

"Want to shower first?" he asked, turning toward me with the shirt.

I shook my head and closed my eyes as he knelt before me. With gentle fingers, he removed my blouse and bra, and slipped the shirt over my head. I fell back onto the soft mattress, and he shimmied my skirt down my legs.

"Under the covers, Giada."

I blinked away the sleep that had begun taking me under again. "Gotta text Mother," I said, crawling under the comforter Logan held back for me.

"Already did."

My face hit my pillow, and I groaned, the softness and warmth of my blankets drawing me under.

Sudden fear of sleep, of nightmares, jolted me awake, and I turned my head enough to peer up at him. "Don't leave me," I whispered.

"I'll stay."

Another sigh at his promise, and I drifted away into darkness.

15

STONE

I sprawled in an armchair pulled close to Giada's bed, my focus on her face every second I wasn't group texting Greed, Warden, and Sin. Two of Burtonelli's guards had sat up front in the limo, and the second car along with the Burtonelli's other guard and Sin had gone straight into Boston to help watch over the rest of the family.

Warden—although the judge had screamed about firing Tellier Security while the EMTs wheeled him outdoors, had gone in the chopper.

The other guards along with Sin had gone straight into Boston to check on the Burtonelli's security at the hospital. Leaving that mess to Warden, I settled into the chair and finally closed my eyes.

Having been on high alert for most of the day, I expected to pass the fuck out knowing I could trust Greed to hold the locked-down fort.

No press, no family, no friends other than Burtonelli and his wife, were allowed past the driveway's gate. I expected the news channels had exploded, but couldn't find it in myself to give a shit.

While we'd kept the truth from the FBI about knowing exactly who put out the hit on the Burtonelli family, my brothers and I hadn't had a chance to discuss what to do about it.

Keeping our secret intel quiet seemed appropriate at the time, but I needed to talk to Vigil. Having almost lost the man I'd been hired to protect, never mind his daughter, I'd about had enough.

Pop's voice echoed in my head all fucking day long, and keeping the shit of my brain from showing on my face had wiped me out.

No good. Failure.

Perhaps allowing the FBI to take over would be best. Burtonelli had fired Tellier Security—even though his house guards had begged—insisted we continue on regardless of the judge's rants until the family all returned home and things calmed down.

Warden had downright ignored the judge's words and climbed into the chopper before takeoff.

He wouldn't allow the events of the day to tarnish his company's reputation. He would stick like stink on shit unless Burtonelli ordered the law to physically remove him.

I let out a heavy exhale and focused on Giada's face. I'd dimmed the overheads enough she could sleep but I could keep watch over her. She hadn't left my side all day, hanging onto me as though I was her anchor in the stormy seas of the day's events.

Even though I'd failed at being the knight in shining armor she seemed to think of me as, I couldn't help the sense of satisfaction her trust and taking comfort in my presence brought.

It was almost enough to do away with Pop's voice, but not quite.

She whimpered and rolled, and I sat forward, watching as emotions flitted over her face in sleep. Furrowed brow. Downturned lips. Cheek twitches. Another whimper.

"Logan," she muttered in her sleep, and the need to comfort her brought me to my feet.

I stripped down and slid beneath her blankets, gently pulling her into my arms.

Lilacs and vanilla swarmed over me as I pressed my lips against her hair. "Shh."

She let out a shuddered sigh and clutched at me, her breathing regulating within seconds.

I closed my eyes and soaked in her trust. Her scent. The warmth of her body with a mere t-shirt between our chests. The truth of exhaustion rolled over me as I realized my dick didn't even twitch.

Knowing Greed sat downstairs and the family's guard had second watch, I meditated on quiet and peace, clearing my mind so sleep would come. At least that part of my self-control still sat intact in my goddamn head.

———

I woke quickly, alert—same as every morning— taking stock of my surroundings, the sounds and scents.

Silence met my ears. Coffee brewed somewhere far away.

I lay facing Giada, my arms still around her.

And my dick was hard, pressed against the inside of her thigh.

Fuck.

I wasn't about to pull away and wake her, though.

Makeup from the day before still smeared over Giada's face, and I cursed myself for not helping her clean up before going to bed. A sigh parted her lips, snagging my gaze, and she shifted, rubbing her soft skin against my aching dick.

Her long eyelashes fluttered—and her eyes opened. She blinked twice, focusing on my face.

"Hey," I whispered, dancing my fingertips down her spine.

"Mmm." She rubbed her lips together and arched her back, stretching, blinking again as my dick jerked against her thigh. Her eyes widened, pupils dilating.

Goddamn, this woman.

I had zero control when it came to Giada Burtonelli. Zero. Zilch. Not a fucking ounce of the self-control I'd honed over my many years of karate and meditation.

A soft smile flitted over her lips as she pressed closer once more, all sweet curves and sleepy warmth.

Fuck it.

I took her mouth, morning breath be damned, losing myself within a heartbeat of her tongue sliding along mine.

Rolling her beneath me had her sighing around our fused lips, and I settled between her spread thighs.

My dick leaked onto the sheets, and I tore myself away, sitting back on my haunches.

I gathered the hem of her shirt in my hands and paused.

She sat up, helping me rid her of the rumpled t-shirt before shimmying out of her panties.

Planking over her, I took her mouth again, and groaned as she wrapped her long legs around me and pulled me closer.

"Need you," she whispered against my mouth.

I'd gone beyond need, and nearly busted a nut while sliding deep inside her wet warmth with one slow thrust.

I cradled her face in my hands, breathing her in, tasting her, memorizing every sensation of softness, slick tightness, whispered sighs and moans.

Fucking heaven. Perfection.

Mine.

I made love to Giada, slow enough to drive us both insane, and we climaxed together, our hearts pounding between the skin and bone separating them.

16

GIADA

A shudder rippled over me, an aftershock of the most intense orgasm of my life, one brought on slowly. Gently. Logan hadn't fucked me, he'd made love to me, and holy hell, did my body respond.

My emotions were tangled in a mess, too.

Growing love for him battled my loyalty to my family and a father who would never approve of Logan Stone.

His heavy body draped over me began to steal my breath, and I tapped his back where I'd dug my fingernails in moments earlier. "Can't breathe."

"Sorry," he muttered, rolling away, his cock slipping from my body.

I moved with him, throwing my leg over his, keeping him close as I could—for as long as I could.

It wouldn't last, I knew.

Father would be home sooner than later—

I jerked upright and hurried to my dresser.

"Phone's over here," Logan said, spinning me back around.

Cum slid down my thighs, but I couldn't be bothered to care. I grabbed my cell off the bed stand and swiped the screen on.

Mother: **Marisa out of surgery. Doctor expects full recovery.**

I choked on a sob and sank to the edge of the bed, tears welling in my eyes. "She's going to be okay."

Logan wrapped his arms around me, and I let him hold me one last time.

We'd had a moment to live the fantasy that would haunt me forever, and I took every last second of comfort I could from his arms while I had the chance.

———

Father and Mother returned in early afternoon, and for once, he didn't bark or bitch at me while making his way up to their bedroom. Mother got him settled before coming back out, dark circles under her eyes, her shoulders slumped.

After catching me up on details concerning my sister in the ICU and her plans to return later in the day—which I argued over—Mother shut herself in their bedroom to shower and catch a small nap.

Logan and Greed took off for a few hours, leaving my family in the care of two of our family guards. The third still sat at the hospital with Marisa.

Silence settled over the house, and I roamed aimlessly, unable to focus on anything, even reading. I missed Cristian's laughter. Hell, I even missed the golden girl's meek presence.

The house was too big, too empty, the opposite of my heart and mind. Depression crept along the edges of my conscious, and I expected I'd be living with that defeating enemy for some time.

Greed returned around dinner time—alone, unfortunately.

"He'll be back in the morning," he said, winking while strolling in the front door while I'd glanced behind him.

My face heated, and I lifted my chin as though I didn't have a clue what he was talking about.

Bummed even more, I sauntered toward the kitchen, my empty stomach needing something even though I didn't have any desire to eat.

Mother returned a few hours later, once visiting hours ended, and we settled in the living room with glasses of wine, something I hadn't done with her in years. She still appeared exhausted, circles under her eyes and all, but the tension had left her shoulders.

"They're going to keep her sedated for a few more days, but the swelling has already gone down considerably. They're hopeful there won't be any permanent brain damage."

True relief rushed through me. I might not care for my sister most of the time, but I had no wish for her to suffer any long term effects from the shooting.

"How are you holding up?"

My focus jerked toward my mother. I couldn't remember the last time she'd cared enough to ask. "I'm thoroughly wrecked. An emotional overloaded basket case. Can't sleep. Don't want to eat. Depressed..."

A sad smile lifted Mother's lips, and the empathy, the feelings of being in the same boat, eased the ache in my heart the slightest bit.

"I see the way you look at him."

LYNN BURKE

My heart stuttered and kicked back into gear with a small shot of adrenaline. I sipped to hide sudden nervousness. "Hmm?"

"Logan Stone," Mother said quietly, her focus unwavering from my face as she lifted her glass to her lips. "I see the way he looks at you, too."

Good fucking God—Mother couldn't keep a damn thing from my father.

"Oh?" I managed to squeak.

"I also saw the way he followed you out of the hall yesterday. Where were going, anyway?"

"Bathroom," I half-choked and cleared my throat before taking a big gulp of wine.

Mother hadn't ever been too intuitive, but perhaps her motherly instinct was working overtime after losing one of her babies and almost losing a second.

"Your father will disown you if he learns of the affair."

I steeled my face to remain impassive. "I'm not having an affair with Logan Stone."

One of her unpainted eyebrows arched as she sipped again. "There are cameras throughout the entire house now, Giada. Your father's men are very loyal to him—but with his health right now, one of the guards brought the information to me instead."

"What information?"

"That Logan Stone exited your bedroom this morning right after his shift began."

I opened my mouth, but Mother held up her hand.

"Don't bother. The guard rewound to the night before when he'd carried you up there. Greed shut you both in—and that door didn't open again until this morning."

"I asked him to stay because I was scared half to death."

Mother studied me long enough I shifted beneath her stare and finally focused on my wine for another healthy swig. "I have to tell your father."

The blood drained from my face. "There's nothing to tell him."

"Mr. Stone isn't the man for you, Giada." She offered a sad smile.

"As if I don't know that," I said with a snorted exhale. Story of my fucking life. "You don't have anything to worry about, Mother. I'm stuck here, bored out of my skull—can you blame me for finding entertainment where I can?"

Her lips pursed. "Perhaps it's time you looked elsewhere."

We sat in silence and finished our wine.

I didn't ask after Father who hadn't made an appearance all day. A visiting nurse had come onboard fulltime to care for him, thank fuck, since I would have loathed having to do so.

"Well," Mother said while pushing up from the couch across from me, "I've had just about enough for the day. I'll see you at breakfast."

I nodded and offered my cheek when she bent to kiss me goodnight.

She would tell Father—of that, I had no doubt.

Creeping upstairs a few minutes later, I strained my ears, listening for Father's raised voice, and I didn't stop until an hour had passed, and I lay in my bed, burying my face in the pillow Logan had used the night before.

I decided once more, regardless of Marisa, I needed to get away, the sooner the better.

17

STONE

Even though we still had the hit out on Arturo, Vigil had Devil anonymously send the FBI everything we had on Arturo Martínez and the threats he'd made on Judge Burtonelli.

The media played the attempted murderer off as a left-wing nutjob. The judge's campaign manager made a little speech outside the hospital a few hours before Burtonelli got released, stating that he would be back on the campaign trail in a matter of days, that nothing and no one would keep him from making Massachusetts a better state.

"Nailing his own fucking coffin shut," Greed muttered to me before taking off for a few hours.

Putting his remaining family in the ground with him, I couldn't help but think while starting my jaunt around the property before settling in for the next eight hours. While I couldn't blame the judge for not backing down—can't let a fucker like Arturo win— my gut didn't like it. Not one fucking bit.

His daughter owned my goddamn soul. No question.

Fuck, just the sight of her when I finally walked through the front door stole my damn breath. She hurried through the archway on the left, her hair in a messy bun, no makeup, a soft-looking sweater hanging off one shoulder, skinny jeans, and fluffy slippers.

My dick took interest—until I lifted my focus back up to her face. She didn't bother trying to hide the pain she felt.

"You okay?" I asked, dropping my overnight bag on the floor and meeting her halfway across the foyer.

Tears welled in her eyes as she peered up at me.

Christ, this woman...

Unable to help myself, I pulled her against my chest, my own aching with the need to make things right for her, to make her smile so I could bask in the beauty of it.

"Marisa?"

"Stable."

Thank fuck. "Your dad?"

"Miserable bastard," she muttered, pulling back enough to peer up at me. "He's still eating breakfast in the dining room, and I had to escape."

Voices raised from deeper in the house, but my spidey-sense lay quiet. "I don't blame you."

I tucked a strand of hair behind her ear, brushing along her jawline with my thumb, but she stepped back, shoving her hands in her pockets before I could kiss the sadness off her downturned lips.

"Mother knows," she whispered.

"What?"

"That you spent the night in my room. One of the guards told her."

Shit. "Your dad know?"

Giada shook her head and rubbed her lips together while glancing away. "Mother hasn't told him yet—but she will. Or maybe that's what all the bitching in there is about."

Another muffled holler reached us.

"I'll handle it."

Giada blew an unsteady breath past her parted lips. "You'd be better off leaving—accepting the fact Father fired you guys after the shooting."

"He apologized to Warden while at the hospital,"

I told her. "Thanked him, even, for sticking with him overnight."

Giada blinked, her eyes widening. "I've never heard my father apologize for *anything*."

My lips twitched. "Guess he had enough of a scare to set his head on straight."

She snorted. "Won't last."

Mutterings and shuffling sounded from the archway announcing her parents' arrival, and Giada offered me a quick smile before fleeing upstairs.

I grabbed my bag and slipped into the control closet, taking off my jacket to hang across the back of the chair. A quick look at the screens showed Giada disappear into her room—and the judge enter the foyer, his wife at his side.

She fussed with his sling.

"Leave me be!" he barked, his voice echoing through the cavernous foyer and closet door I'd left open.

I stepped out to greet him.

Burtonelli's lips thinned as he noticed me, his cheeks mottled, rage in his eyes.

"Sir," I greeted him. "How are you feel—"

"I pay you good money to protect my family, not fuck my daughter!" Spittle flew from his lips.

"It isn't—"

"You're nothing, do you hear me?" He raised his finger, pointing at my face, and I fought to keep from fisting my hands at my sides. "Nothing! Low class."

The Burtonelli's head of security appeared at the top of the stairs, his brow furrowed as he glanced between the judge and me.

I turned back to the judge. "Sir, if you would let me explain—"

"You're not a good enough man for a Burtonelli —even if she is a rebellious whore!"

"Do not call her that." I shot back, having had enough.

"She's my goddamn daughter, I can call her whatever the hell I want!"

Fuck it. Warden might be my best friend, my brother, but Giada came first.

"You ought to be proud of that girl," I said, step-ping closer, allowing him to see my rage in my eyes. "She's worked her *ass* off to make a name for herself in the fashion industry, living a fake-ass life just like every politician chasing their dream, bent on gaining people's admiration and support."

The judge sputtered, but I wasn't done.

"That woman is strong as fuck. She chose to make her own money rather than ride the coat tails of the one man who should have been there for her.

Supported her. Encouraged her to seek out her dreams. Giada is self-motivated. Driven. That woman has bigger balls than you,—"

"Get. Out."

"—Judge Burtonelli. Perhaps you ought to step back and reevaluate the gift of her."

"Get out of my house right now!"

The guard came down the stairs, and I kept an eye on him in my periphery. "Stone," he said quietly.

"I'm not leaving here until I speak with Giada."

"You have *any* contact with my daughter," Burtonelli spit, "and you can forget about that little deal I made with your president."

I didn't give two shits about that deal Vigil had made with the asshole in front of me, but nothing good would come from an altercation. I had Giada's cell number—I'd never used it, but that would change.

Without another word, I grabbed my bag and jacket off the back of the closet chair and started toward the front door.

"You tell Drew Tellier I'm no longer in need of his services," Burtonelli said as I pulled open the door.

A conversation I did not look forward to.

I slammed the door shut behind me.

18

GIADA

I heard every word—heard Logan slam the door behind him. My throat swelled tight, and I eased my bedroom door shut, resting my forehead against it.

No one had ever stuck up for me in the way he had. No one had sung my praises beyond my beauty and ability to move in front of a camera.

What Father saw as stubborn rebellion, Logan saw as positive traits. He saw the real me, the motivated woman driven to live her own life. He hardly knew me, but he *knew* me.

And yet he left at the mention of a broken deal made between my father and the Vipers.

Obviously, his feelings for me weren't enough to trump the brotherhood he'd been a part of for over ten years. A sob caught in my throat as twin tears slid down my cheeks.

"Giada Burtonelli!" Father's voice sounded outside my room, and I jolted back from the door, wrapping my arms around myself. He pushed into my room without knocking.

"You've gone too far, young lady!"

I swiped away another tear I couldn't keep from falling. My chest ached—fucking hurt like hell.

"Sleeping with that man!" Father actually spit on my bedroom floor as Mother appeared in the doorway behind him. "He got what he wanted from my daughter the whore and left without a fight. Used you like the piece of trash you are."

I shut Father out, refusing to let his words heap atop the hurt Logan's leaving had caused—nothing could hurt worse than that. Father cursed me a few dozen times, reiterating all the negativity I'd been fed my entire life.

Worthless. A stain on the Burtonelli name. Facts I fought against every minute of the day.

"You will stay away from that man—those Vipers, am I clear, Giada?"

I sank onto the edge of my bed and nodded just to shut him the hell up. Logan had made his choice, so obeying *that* order would be easy.

"I so much as hear a whisper of the Burtonelli name attached to that outlaw gang because of you, and you're gone, do you hear me? You'll no longer be a part of this family. I'll disown you. Strip you of your inheritance."

I nodded again.

He spun away—thank fuck—and I held up a hand as Mother rushed toward me.

"Don't."

She pulled up short, her eyes welled. "Baby—"

"I want to be alone." My heart lay dead in my chest, unmoved by the emotion wrinkling her face. My mother, the one who should have protected me, who should have stood up for me with the mother's love I'd seen her show for both Cristian and Marisa.

She could have kept quiet about what the guard told her. She could have chosen to let me find some happiness while being forced to live under their roof. She could have loved me enough to choose *me* over Father just once.

Instead, she'd chosen him—same as always.

The door snicked shut quietly behind her, and I let out one hell of a big breath.

There was no way in hell I could stay. It was time to revisit my teenage years, the wild days of learning how to be sneaky as hell in getting what I wanted.

Freedom.

It would come at a cost, but one I was more than willing to pay.

———

Fab, the doll, agreed to help me out. He'd heard all about the hellish home I'd grown up in, and we'd bonded over similar treatment in our childhoods. Upon coming out, both his parents had ridiculed him, called him a sinner, told him he would rot in hell. He'd escaped the day he turned eighteen and hadn't ever looked back.

Time for me to do the same.

I waited until my parents left to visit Marisa in the hospital—leaving one guard to watch over me and the entire house since Tellier Security had been sent on their merry way. Needing to pack light, I only stuffed one duffle bag with clothes, my eReader, and vibrator—and chargers for both.

Sneakers tied tight and hair in a ponytail, I nibbled on a fingernail while adrenaline rushed through me. I peered out my bedroom window on the second floor overlooking the estate gate and driveway. Fab pulled up in his BMW a half-hour later, and my chewed-to-the-quick fingernail stung like a bitch.

"Here we go," I said, breathless and pulse thrumming.

He pressed the buzzer, and I waited, pulling my duffle bag's straps over my shoulders like a backpack.

Fab was far enough away I couldn't make out his mouth moving in conversation with the guard who must be speaking with him through the intercom. He eventually climbed out of the car, slammed the door as though pissed, and leaned down to press the button, his free hand flying—proof he ran at the mouth.

I actually giggled.

He stepped back from the intercom, rounded the front of his car, arms crossed, as he stared down the house.

Seconds later, the guard exited below me and stalked down the driveway toward him.

I grabbed my coat and booked it downstairs and out the back, my heart in my throat, adrenaline rushing and shaking me like a leaf as my sneakers slapped the treads.

No one sat in front of the monitors—and last the guard had seen was me shutting myself up in my bedroom after Logan had left me behind. Unless he watched back through the few minutes Fab had taken him away from the screens, I had a good few hours before my parents returned home and found me missing from my room—if they even thought to check on me.

I sprinted through Mother's manicured gardens, leaping over intentionally placed rocks and dried, brittle bushes. Cold air rushed into my lungs, and even though I only had a hundred or so yards to run, my legs burned before I reached the back of the property. I climbed the old pine in order to scale the wall surrounding my parents' estate, but I'd done it enough times as a teenager that it came back easy.

Up and over.

Boom.

The street lay a few yards away, and I shot Fab a text letting him know I'd made my escape. Two minutes later, my cell phone powered off and tucked away, my savior came around the corner. I tossed my shit onto his back seat and slid into the warm interior, sweat still beaded on my brow and between my breasts.

I slumped, my head tipping back against the seat as I let out an enormous breath, the adrenaline still slamming my heart in my chest. "Thank you."

He giggled. "That poor man didn't know what to do with me.'

I chuckled, and turned my head toward him, still boneless although the adrenaline shakes took over. "You're the best, Fab."

A quick wink of real eyelashes instead of fake slathered with mascara, and he squeezed my hand. "So what's your plan?"

"Bank first, then the airport."

"Where are you headed?"

"I'm going to the one place no one would ever think to look for me."

"Your cousin's?"

"Oh fuck no!" I almost choked on a laugh. "Good one, though. No, I'm hopping the first flight to Vegas."

He snickered and turned onto the main road. "You hate Vegas."

"Exactly." I closed my eyes and focused on breathing the shakes away. While excited over finally making a true escape, my heart ached over the whole Logan affair—even more so than leaving Marisa behind.

I could eventually make contact with her, and perhaps, with time, I'd forget about the alpha biker who had rocked my world.

Surely there were others out there—and having had a taste of that fairytale mc romance come to life, nothing else would do.

I hoped another man could fill his shoes, but I highly doubted it.

19

STONE

After leaving the Burtonellis, I went straight to the club intending to have a few shots of whiskey—and swore when I saw Warden's truck in the lot.

"The fuck is he doing here this early in the morning?" I grumbled to myself while parking. I climbed out, slamming the driver door behind me. A gust of wind slapped me in the face, and I hunched in my jacket, hurrying to the club's entrance.

Only a handful of other vehicles sat in the parking area, two of which I knew belonged to prospects months away from getting patched in.

Sin sat right inside the door, leaning back in his chair, arms crossed.

"The fuck is going on?" I asked, shutting out the winter wind behind me.

"Meeting in Vigil's office," he said, motioning toward the closed door with his chin. "Two prospects got into it with knives last night after you went home."

"The fuck for?"

"One of the whores."

"Stupid fucks."

"Warden and I were on the way to meet up with a client when Vigil called him in."

Since I wasn't a Viper officer, I couldn't just waltz on in and interrupt their meeting. "Fuck." I scrubbed a hand down over my face. "How long they been in there."

"Over an hour."

"Shit."

"The fuck you doing here?" Sin asked, righting his chair, frowning as though remembering at that second where I ought to be.

"Burtonelli fired us."

"Thought Warden took care of that shit when he was in the hospital with the fucker."

I sank into a chair across from him. "That shit was. This is new shit."

One of Sin's brows arched. "The fuck?"

"I fucked his daughter. He found out. End of story."

"Oh holy shit!" Sin chuckled. "Greed said you had it bad for her—how the fuck you get in her panties?"

I shot a glare at him, and his smile faded in a blink.

The office door opened, keeping me from spouting off at my brother, and I hopped back up, eyeing the two prospects shuffling out.

Warden followed on their heels. "Stone? Why the hell aren't you at the Burtonellis?"

I nodded him back toward the office. "We need to chat."

"The fuck is this?" Vigil said, getting up from behind his desk when he caught sight of me following Warden back into his office.

"I made a poor fucking decision," I got right to it like ripping off a goddamn batter while shutting the door behind me. "A mistake that cost you the favor Burtonelli owed the Vipers."

"Fuck." Vigil glared while settling back in his chair. "Sit the fuck down."

I did as told, directly across from him.

His glare reminded me of Pop's, and I fought off

the need to defend myself. "The fuck did you do, Stone?"

"Fucked his daughter."

"Goddamnitalltofuckinghell..."

"I'd love to blame her," I said, "but no woman controls my dick."

Warden snorted. "Then you haven't met the right woman."

I'd met the right woman, alright—I just had to find a way of making her mine without creating even more of a mess. If that was even fucking possible.

"It was a stupid fucking mistake. I'm not normally distracted like that."

Warden made a nose of agreement in his throat.

"Goddamnit." Vigil stretched his neck side to side, his gaze flitting around the office while he continued to scowl. "Well, it's no real skin off my back. Woulda been nice to have a Senator owe the Vipers a favor, but that kind of offense..." He shook his head, lips pursed.

"Sorry, Vigil."

"He can your ass?"

I nodded and glanced at Warden.

"Don't worry about it," Warden said, his waiving me off and furrowing my brow.

"Don't worry about it?" I shot back. "The fuck,

man? Burtonelli's pissed. You think he isn't going to throw your company—your fucking *name*—into the shitter?"

"You claiming her?"

Warden's question, rather than agreed concern, snapped my jaw shut.

He leaned against the wall, arms crossed, smug as a fucking kid with a pocketful of stolen candy when I didn't respond. "Is Giada yours or not?"

I glanced at Vigil.

The fucker grinned at me. "She *is* one tasty-looking morsel. All the brothers think so."

A muscle in my jaw ticked. Fuck, I hated his ribbing.

"Stone's got himself an old lady." Vigil slapped his palm on the desk and stood up. "It's too fucking early, but I need a drink."

He strode out to the club, simple as that—his word law—and I met Warden's gaze.

"She doesn't know," I told him.

"She will, you stubborn prick. Come on, brother," he said, clasping my shoulder as I stood. "I already reschedule my meeting for this morning, so let's go get fucked up with Vigil. Then we'll talk about going to rescue your old lady."

"It isn't even nine in the morning," I argued, following him out of the office.

"It's five o'clock fucking somewhere," he shot over his shoulder.

The man had a point—but just one to calm me the fuck down. I had a woman to get in contact with so I could make things right.

One turned into two. Two turned into three, and until I came to my fucking senses, I found myself sprawled on one of the club's couches, a full on party rocking the house.

My head fucking hurt.

I pinched the bridge of my nose, cursing myself from hell to heaven and back again. The fuck had I done? I rarely drank like a fish, but my laughing brothers had decided I needed to let loose. Give up control for a change.

I'd done that with Giada, and look where it had gotten me.

No. What I *really* needed to do was get in contact with her, stake my claim, and get her the hell outta there.

Pulling myself into a sitting position cranked my headache into full force, and I groaned.

Stupid fuck.

My cell vibrated against my ass, and I pulled it out.

Burtonelli.

Frowning, I swiped to answer even though I wouldn't be able to hear much over the thumping music and ruckus of brothers having a kickass Friday night.

"Stone!" I heard his bark clear as a fucking bell and his wife's sobs in the background. "Where the hell is my daughter?"

Daughter. I blinked at the fuzziness in my brain. Marisa still lay sedated ... *Giada.*

Oh, fuck.

"She's gone," Burtonelli screamed over the line, "and if the authorities find her with you, so help me God—"

Fuckin hell.

My woman had gone missing.

20

GIADA

I'd turned my cell phone off, but decided to text Mother once I landed myself a hotel room. Yes, her treatment of me had hardened my heart toward her, but I didn't want her worrying I'd been kidnapped by leaving without a trace. I didn't tell her where I'd gone, just asked her to keep me updated on Marisa's progress.

The second the text went through, I shut the phone back off.

For two whole days, I binged on junk food, take out, and raunchy e-books. My vibrator got one hell of a work out, but release didn't bring satisfaction. I craved dick—Logan's dick specifically.

He'd ruined me for anyone else I'd decided—easily accepted without giving anyone else a shot.

Monday morning, I woke with his name on my lips, visions lingering from my vivid dream of him planking over me, his blue eyes open and unshielded, peering into mine.

Goddamn, I missed that man even though my chest still ached over not being enough for him.

Steeling myself against disappointment, I grabbed my cell and powered it on, blinking and rubbing the sleep from my eyes while waiting for the screen to come to life.

Did he even know I'd taken off? Did he care?

Twenty-two missed calls. Three text messages— Fab making sure I'd arrived safely, Mother ordering me to call her, and Logan doing the same.

I ignored the transcribed voice messages from Father and Mother, clicking straight on Logan's in order to hear his voice.

"Giada. I'm fucking worried sick—please call me. Your mother won't tell me where you've gone, but says you're safe. I know why you took off—I'd have done the same—I just don't understand why you didn't tell me. Why you haven't called. Fuck, Giada."

I imagined him scrubbing his hand over his face at his groan.

"Please. I can't fucking stand this silence. I need to know you're okay."

A twinge of hope snagged its claws into my heart —to call or not to call? He cared, but only enough to make sure I was okay? Could I stand even more disappointment?

I chewed the inside of my lip and shuffled to the bathroom to take care of business, debating over hearing his voice again or getting crushed when he didn't tell me to come home—to him.

We had no understanding.

He'd left without a fight, leaving me to face the fire alone. He'd broken that promise he'd made to be there for me.

I powered my cell off and shoved it back in the bed stand drawer.

———

The back of my neck tingled, raising the shorter hairs at my nape escaping my ponytail. A baseball hat sat low on my brow, and I wore big ass sunglasses while out in public—just in case. I doubted anyone could hurt my father by taking me out, but they didn't know that.

Best to be safe.

I stopped strolling along the sidewalk and pretended to window shop, checking out the people behind me. While I felt like someone watched me, I didn't see anyone suspicious. One heavy exhale, and I started off once more, telling myself to get a grip.

It had been a week since I'd left home, and I still couldn't decide what I wanted to do with my suddenly wide-open future.

Fab had hooked me up with those two photographers—both in spring which still lay a couple of months off, and I really didn't want to return to the east coast before then.

I'd put my condo up for sale, and had asked Fab to ready it for showings. If I got an offer that looked promising, I'd be forced to return home to pack up all my shit.

No one needed to know, though. Sneak back east, get shit done, take off once more.

But to where? And for how long?

Indecision, the hazy future I couldn't seem to focus on, heaped on top of the shit of depression I'd been slumping under since Cristian's death. I didn't know what I wanted to do other than see Logan— yet, I wanted to avoid him, too.

He'd called twice more in the week since I'd been gone, both times a simple, "Please call me", tempting me to the point of hovering my fingertip over the green call button.

The hairs on my nape stuck straight up as a shiver licked down my spine—and *so* not the pleasant sort.

A man approached me, and although he wore dark sunglasses, I swore he bee-lined right for me. Tall. Dark hair. Scruffy beard. Jeans, nice boots, and a light zipper jacket against the cooler morning air.

Not anyone I knew.

I slipped into a café, my heart in my throat, and kept my back to the door while stepping into line.

No bell tinkled to announce a new patron as it had done for me, and I finally flitted a glance over my shoulder—no sunglasses man.

Feeling like a fool, I ordered a coffee and sat in the corner where I could see the sidewalk through the front windows. Three sips in, and sunglasses man ambled past, glancing into the café while walking by.

Adrenaline shot through me again, and I grasped my coffee cup in my hands to keep them from trembling.

He could have gone some place and was simply making his way back.

You wish.

Ten minutes later, I caught sight of him across

the street. He hung in front of a store front as I had done, window shopping. Or did he?

I pulled my cell out of my purse, my entire body shaking like crazy.

"Giada!" Logan answered before it even rang on my end.

"Logan—some guy is following me, and I'm freaking the fuck out!" I whispered, my heart in my throat.

"Where are you?"

"At some café in Vegas."

"Fuck."

"What should I do?" I bit down on my lip as he swore again.

"Call the cops—or go straight to the station if it's close by."

"I have no clue where it is."

"Do you know him?"

I checked the guy out again—he stood unmoving. "No. Never seen him before in my life."

"What's he look like? What's he wearing?"

I described what I could, just knowing Logan was on the other end of the line calming me enough I could think straight.

"Keep me on the line," he said, "and look up the closest station."

I did as told, my fingers shaking. "Three blocks."

"How far away is your car?"

"I-I walked."

"Are you with anyone—is there anyone at the café you can ask to walk you to the station?"

"I'm here alone," I said, doing a quick scan around me. "There's one woman here by herself reading. I-I'll ask her."

"I'm staying on the line with you, Giada. Don't hang up."

"Okay."

"Tell her what's going on and ask her to walk with you. Don't hang up with me until you're at the station, got it?"

"Okay." I grabbed my purse and took my mug to the counter before approaching the woman.

She glanced up from her book and smiled as I got closer and lowered my cell in front of me.

"Hey." I swallowed, my knees shaking like crazy. "So, I have a huge favor to ask..."

21

STONE

I shut myself in my dojo's office the second Giada's call came through. Emotions I'd never experienced in my life crashed against me like a goddamn tidal wave, slamming my heart in my chest at the first words I'd heard from her lips in over a week.

Powerless, I paced my office while talking to her, getting what information I could about the fucker stalking her, my free hand fisting and un-fisting with the need to strike a heavy bag.

My mind cursed non-fucking stop as I strained to make out her conversation with the woman.

"She's coming with me," Giada finally said in my ear.

"Walk fast—don't stop for anything, you hear me?"

"Yes, sir."

I'd never heard Giada's voice sound so meek, and it scared the shit out of me. My strong girl with a backbone of steel sounded like a frightened child—it fucking killed me.

A bell tinkled distantly, and muffled sounds of traffic sounded immediately after.

"I really appreciate this," I heard Giada tell the woman, her voice far away—not holding the cell to her ear.

"Not a problem. Glad I could help." The woman had an accent—French, perhaps.

I forced myself to stand in one spot, eyes closed and breathing deeply as the seconds passed. "Giada?"

She didn't answer.

"Giada!" I hollered.

"I'm here... One block down."

"Is he following?"

The seconds of hesitation while she glanced around twisted my guts into a tight knot. "I-I don't see him, no."

"Keep going—and don't hang up until you're inside the station. I want an officer to drive you back to your hotel where you're going to pack up your shit and get your ass home."

"I'm not going back there, Logan."

"Not to your parents," I snipped. "To *my* home."

"Oh!" She gasped as though smiling and fumbled with her phone. "Logan!" Her muffled shriek knifed my heart.

"Giada!" I glanced down at my phone—the call had ended.

I hit redial—straight to voicemail.

"No!" I hit redial again—fucking voicemail. "Giada! Goddamnit, Giada!"

My hand shook while dialing 911, and I tore out of my office, gunning for the club.

———

"Got it," Devil said, and I hurried to peer over his shoulder at the laptop he had on Vigil's desk and the open page of the hotel registration she'd made. "She checked in there on Friday, late."

"Show me the café and station she was walking toward."

Seconds later, the map showed onscreen, and I studied it while running through what I knew. Giada had never made it to the station—nor had a woman with a French accent with any story of assault.

"Get me a ticket to Vegas," I told Devil.

"I'll go with you," Ryker said from behind me.

I nodded while watching Devil's fingers fly over the keys. "Make that two tickets," I told him.

"I'll call the Vegas chapter," Vigil said from behind his desk. "Get them on it while you're enroute."

"Appreciate it."

It could have been random—some psycho stalking Giada—I just knew whatever had happened wasn't good. She'd have called me to let me know if she was okay. The French woman would have reported a kidnapping—unless she'd been unable to for some reason. My suspicious nature suggested the woman had been in on it, but the chances of that lay close to nil.

The not knowing, the inability to protect Giada raged inside me like a caged, enraged polar bear. Especially since the call I'd put through to the Vegas P.D. didn't get me anywhere.

No evidence of a kidnapping, but at least I'd been able to file a missing person's report—but Vegas averaged five to seven missing adults per goddamn day.

I didn't have high expectations in their help finding her.

I tried her cell countless times before boarding the plane, and every time it went straight to voice-mail. Ryker slept like a baby during the six-plus hour flight, but my mind refused to quiet. Scenarios continued to badger my mind, amping up the acid in my stomach to the point I asked the flight attendant for some antacids.

My stomach properly chalked up, and my nerves settled to steel, we exited the plane with our carry-ons.

Klingon, the Vegas Viper's chapter President met us at the airport. He stuck out his hand to Ryker who looked at the offer of welcome and raised an eyebrow.

"Still a cold, little cunt, I see," Klingon said with a laugh.

"Fuck off," Ryker muttered. "You know I hate to be touched."

I stepped forward to shake Klingon's hand. The dude was hairy as fuck, his size and dark scowl put Ryker's to shame.

"Grew up in Southie with me," Ryker said as we followed Klingon to his car.

Yes, Klingon as in the Star Trek species. Intimidating as fuck. People took care to swing a wide berth when we approached. But I supposed three pissed off men in Viper's cuts alone would have done the same.

I filled Klingon in as we drove to his club—most of which Vigil had already shared with him.

"I've got a room set up for you back behind the club," he said, his voice deep and dark as his piercing eyes. "Isn't much, but it's yours for however long you need."

"Appreciate it," I told him while scanning the dark scenery beyond the passenger window.

"My club is your club," he continued. "You need my brothers' help, it's yours."

Unlike the club back home, the Vegas boys didn't have an enclosed lot. The building housing their club sprawled not far off an exit, more like a small shopping plaza lit up like a football stadium on a Friday night.

Bikes lined the front of the main section— looked like a hopping party.

"Gets a little loud," Klingon warned us while parking. "Can't promise you won't hear it out back."

"Not a problem." I climbed out when he parked and grabbed my bag from Ryker who'd had it on the back seat beside him.

Our entrance drew a lot of attention. Drinks and hollers of welcome raised as we followed Klingon into his kingdom. While I wasn't in the mood to drink, there wasn't much I could do to look for Giada right then.

I took the cold bottle pressed into my hand and got pulled into backslapping hugs countless times before making it into Klingon's office.

Ryker greeted a few guys by name, but he'd been around a hell of a lot longer than I had.

The Vegas Vipers had already heard about my woman's disappearance, and over a dozen offered personal assistance to help in whatever way they could.

A handful of Klingon's officers followed us into his office, and we sat at the huge round table dominating the room. Shutting the office door behind us didn't muffle the noise of the main room entirely, but at least I could think straight.

Klingon sat at the head and leaned forward, hands clasped on the table. "Tell my boys everything —then we're going to figure out what the fuck happened to your woman and get her back."

———

The Vegas Vipers had connections—but no one in their back pocket had heard jack shit about Giada Burtonelli. No whiff, no hint of a lead rose in the day after our arrival. The police proved just as helpful.

Only two of the businesses in the area where I knew she'd disappeared from agreed to let me watch footage of their security cameras during the time our call had cut out. Neither showed what I needed to see.

I retraced her steps from the café toward the station and wondered how the fuck she could have been snatched up without anyone noticing. She'd shrieked my name—someone had to have seen or heard something.

The first time I walked the route, a burned out teen hung on the corner of one road across the street, a cigarette hanging from the corner of his lips. On my second day in Vegas, my second walk of those three blocks, I caught sight of him again and detoured across the street.

"Hey, kid!" I forced a smile, not wanting to scare the shit out of him.

Brow furrowed, he flitted his gaze down over me. "The fuck you want?"

"Just some information." I held up a twenty and a picture of Giada. "This woman disappeared two days ago at ten-seventeen right around this area. Happen to see anything?"

He took the picture rather than the cash. "She's hot as fuck. She yours?"

I ground my molars together. "Have you seen her?"

"Yeah. Maybe."

A shot of adrenaline raced through my heart.

"Dunno." The kid eyed the cash in my hand, and I pulled another twenty from my pocket.

"Tell us what you know, kid." Ryker stepped from behind me, and the youngster glanced at him and the cut he wore—the evidence of who I ran with in the event it turned people off from helping me.

"You guys Vipers?"

I nodded.

The kid swallowed and handed back the picture of Giada. "She had on big sunglasses. Walked with some blonde girl. Right over there." He pointed across the street at the exact spot I figured she'd disappeared. "Van pulled up and stopped for all of three seconds. It pulled away and both women were gone."

Fuck.

"Tell me everything you can remember," I managed through gritted teeth.

Black Chevy cargo van, newer model, but he didn't catch the license plate number.

Rather than head to the police station, I went back to the two businesses with my lead. The second showed a glimpse of a black cargo van making a turn —and a snapshot of a fuzzy plate.

Hope tickled my mind.

I sent the image to Devil, and until he cleaned it up and gave me the information I wanted, my stomach tied itself in knots again. Antacids became my best friend.

Ryker and I sat with Klingon and his VP when Devil's call came through.

"Got it, brother." His voice betrayed his thoughts on the asshole.

"Who?"

"Van is registered to a guy named Jose Santiago." Devil spouted off the address, and I glanced at Klingon.

"I know that fucker." Wariness filled his eyes. "Know the businesses he has his fists into—fucking shoulder deep."

My goddamn stomach burned. "What?' I pushed when he didn't seem to want to elaborate.

"Skin."

Fuck.

Ryker's spewing curses muffled as kill mode settled down over me, shutting down emotions, all distractions. My calm façade slipped into place, leaving me hard as stone, exactly as my brothers had decided to call me.

"Find him," I told Klingon. "Find where the fuck he is."

Ryker eyed me with a hint of wariness in his gaze, a look I'd never seen him give anyone. "We're gonna get her back," he said, but his assurance didn't bolster any hope inside me.

Shut down. Dead inside—and I'd remain that way unless Giada returned to me, whole, healthy, and fucking untouched.

For over an hour, Devil dug and Klingon sniffed around. The Chevy-driving fucker led us to a man named Volkov, the top dog in Vegas. If a rich fucker wanted to purchase a sex slave, he had what you wanted.

The following evening he'd planned a private sale at his estate in western Vegas overlooking conservation land. Hush, hush, but Klingon had known who to prod for the information. His dealings in the black market gave him the eyes and ears needed to dig up the goods.

"Whatcha wanna do?" Klingon asked, sitting back in his chair, his focus on my face.

"Go in and clean the place out."

"If they're buying from him, there's going to be big names. Lots of money. Guards."

"Hit it right the fuck now," Ryker suggested.

I wanted to do the same more than draw my next breath, but I was going to hit the Volkov fucker so goddamn hard, he'd be shut down for good.

"We're going to get eyes on that estate—get everyone entering and leaving on camera from now until tomorrow morning. Then we go in." I stated a fact, not a suggestion.

Klingon eyed me for a few seconds. "You want to take down the ring."

"Fucking right."

A muscle twitched the wild black beard covering his jaw. "We're in."

I nodded once.

"Then let's get started."

22

GIADA

I refused to cry. Life had fucked me up the ass without a trace of lube since New Year's, seemingly hell-bent on burying me.

Well, fuck that, and fuck the fuckers who plucked me off the street like a goddamn weed.

I'm a goddamn fucking rose.

That line whispered loudly in my head over and over, helping to steel my nerves against the situation I'd been tossed into.

When the van had first dropped me and the poor woman who'd agreed to walk me to the police station off in some underground parking area, I envisioned every horror film coming to life before my eyes.

Reality proved ten times worse.

We were led to a dungeon-like room where they finally snipped off the zip ties around our wrists. Cold, damp air chilled me through, my nose stinging from the stench of urine. Typical "I'm gonna die" vibes in every sense, feeding the anxiety clawing in my stomach.

Ten other women sat huddled in the dark. Two got carted off within an hour, five after my new French bestie, Aline, slept for a little while. With no cell, watch, or window, we'd been lost to time.

And for Aline, it had been my fault. Regardless, she clung to me as if to say, "You got me into this shit, you're getting me out of it".

Three younger girls got dumped in with us later, and no one knew for sure what was going on—but some of us had read enough novels to speculate. My speaking the possibilities out loud sent most of the women into psychotic fits. One even passed out.

I decided that until I either stood seconds from meeting my maker—or *owner* as I expected—I would hold onto my shit, thank you very much.

Father hadn't broken me.

The loss of my dear brother hadn't.

I was strong as fuck—had bigger balls than Father, just like Logan had claimed. I would prove him right and hold my chin up until the very end.

Even if it meant sexually servicing some fucker until I could sink a blade into his gullet and escape.

I am strong...

I swallowed against the fear while being led up two flights of stairs with Aline and one other woman. We'd been ordered to remain silent, and I would be that good little girl until the time came for shit to come down.

We came into a massive kitchen—commercial yet fancy as fuck in the morning light streaming through the windows overlooking gardens and the dry desert beyond—and up another flight of servant-like stairs before being shown into a windowless bedroom.

Two bunkbeds. Wooden floors. Connecting bathroom.

On order to strip and shower, I didn't hesitate. Used to being in front of a camera without clothing made it easy, and I hopped in first to wash away the grime from the previous two days.

We'd been given sandwiches while in our prison, which I'd forced down, but the aroma that hit my face when I exited the bathroom wrapped in a towel turned my mouth's water works on full force.

Fettuccini alfredo. Three big bowls with crusty bread—and a damn bottle of Chardonnay.

Okay...

I studied the guard by the door as Aline slipped into the bathroom behind me and the other woman huddled on one of the lower bunks.

A table had been set in the middle of the room while I'd showered, fancy as shit with real silverware and all.

The guard ignored me, but I eyed the fork while sitting my ass down. If someone had wanted to poison me through food, they'd have done it through the damn sandwich, and I expected Buffalo Boy over by the door would only laugh in my face if I brandished a fork as a weapon. There'd been no razor in the bathroom, nothing to wield in self-defense. If it came to that, the fork would have to do.

A girl *might* get lucky.

Hunger and the knowledge I needed to keep up my energy trumped my anxious stomach. I dug in into my meal—and shouldn't have moaned at the first buttery flavor to hit my tongue, but damn, whoever prepared that alfredo knew what the hell they were doing.

The other girl joined me within two minutes, probably waiting to see if I'd start foaming at the lips first before touching the food.

We ate in silence until I licked the bowl clean.

Every. Damn. Smear. The Chardonnay slid down like water, smooth and expensive as hell, without doubt.

Someone wanted us ladies happy.

I could pretend to be so if it meant getting me answers.

A man entered without knocking as Aline came from the bathroom wrapped in a towel identical to mine. She paused in the doorway, and I swirled the wine in my glass as the man studied our faces.

I'd expected a hot as hell dominant male like in my fairytale romance books, some rich fucker who dabbled in sex slaves to pad his empire's bank accounts.

The man before us was little. Squirrely. Clean shaven with a strong jawline and empty, dark eyes, but he didn't scare me. Not one bit. Hell, I had at least three inches on him.

"So is this meant for our enjoyment, or yours?" I asked him, keeping my tone polite. Fake as fuck, exactly as I'd learned from my parents.

His lips twitched. "Giada Burtonelli."

I touched the tip of my finger to my nose even though his men had taken my purse when they'd taken me, so of course he'd know my name. "And you are, sir?"

He chuckled. "Sir. I like that." He turned his focus on the woman seated beside me.

She kept her head down, her shoulders quivering same as when I'd followed her up the stairs.

I glanced at Aline and beckoned her closer with my head. "Come sit, Aline."

Her blonde hair plastered wet to her head shivered along with the rest of her body, but she listened and sat in the empty chair on my other side.

"Eat," I told her quietly and turned my attention back on our captor.

"So." I raised an eyebrow and waited.

He chuckled again. "Once you've eaten—and you've showered," he told our unwashed companion, "someone will be in to help ready the three of you for this evening's festivities."

I could only imagine...

"Festivities." I smiled, ignoring the hairs on my nape rising. "I love a good party."

His dark eyes hardened, and he lowered his chin. I wanted to laugh at his display of badassery, but true fear ate beneath the façade of my face.

"He's going to have fun breaking you," our captor promised, his focus on my eyes.

The sudden urge to pee squeezed my thighs, and my breathing snagged short of a full inhale. I wanted to arch a brow and inquire as to whom he spoke of, but my tongue twisted against the stirring in my stomach.

I managed a smile—and he spun on his heel, leaving the three of us alone once more with Buffalo Boy.

The second the door snicked shut, I slouched, letting out a shuddered breath.

"You're crazy," Aline whispered—and our companion took up crying again.

She'd only eaten half her food, and twisted her hands in her lap, her dirty-blonde hair shielding her face.

"Go shower. Take those minutes of privacy, of freedom," I told her. "You'll feel a bit better. Trust me."

She did as told without speaking a word or looking up from the floor.

I glanced over at Aline reading the fear in her eyes. "You know what this is."

"I do," she whispered.

I nodded, exhaled a heavy sigh once more, and finished my Chardonnay.

———

Someone came to ready us for the "festivities" alright. A man equipped with makeup bags, hair products, and one assistant.

What should have felt like a spa treatment did nothing for my nerves or the two women with me. Plucked and primped as though ready to face a camera, I should have been in my element.

The lack of clothing didn't bother me as much as it did Aline and Dianna—she'd finally given us her name—but keeping my chin high and steps sure while following Buffalo Boy back down the stairs hours later proved one of the most difficult things I'd done in my life.

Through the kitchen, down a hallway—into a narrower hallway where another Buffalo Boy joined us.

A room opened ahead—a wall of dark glass ahead. One-way mirror.

Yup. Fucked.

I imagined the men on the other side of the glass, checking out the butt-naked wares for sale. My knees finally knocked, my hands fisting at my sides as the first guard ordered us to stand side by side in the center of the brightly lit room.

I studied my reflection in the darkened glass,

noting how my chin stayed raised, my shoulders back as my companions cowered.

Bring it on, bitches, I silently told those fuckers inspecting us. *Pay your fee and get me out of here so I can see what I'm up against.*

23

STONE

I wished I'd thought to bring some of Warden's high tech shit along, but Klingon had a boy in the black market hook us up with some good ass shit on short notice. High tech night vision goggles. Two-way radio earpieces we were able to patch Devil into. Fucking tracking devices to slip onto the cars of the fuckers who arrived to pay big cash for sex slaves in the event any managed to escape us.

We had no idea how many men would arrive at the estate. We knew the location and time. Had memorized a grid map of the neighborhood and lay of the conservation land sprawling behind the back of the estate—our best chance for sneaking in.

It meant making our way in the dark through

terrain I wasn't well-acquainted with, but I refused to be intimidated.

Dressed all in black, Ryker, Klingon, another of his guys who used to be a sniper in the Marines, and I snuck into the shadows from where his VP had dropped us off outside the neighborhood.

It took us an hour to swing around to the west of the house and get eyes on the location of where my woman was being held.

Devil had hacked into the mansion's security system—I'd seen her in a room with two other women. I'd seen the guard, the man who'd come to chat with them. My Giada had held his gaze, her lips moving in response to his. She kept her chin up, only one tick of the corner of her lip revealing her distain for the fucker. Not an ounce of fear bled through the face she put on.

Balls of fucking steel. Grim determination, same as me.

If anyone could survive what threatened her, Giada would. If anyone could bust those women out and take down a mere pinkie of the skin trade's body, the Vipers could.

We would.

Two guards, clear as day through our goggles, stood on the back terrace, another two atop the house. All four appeared empty-handed, but in a development with neighbors not too far off, such guns would call unwanted attention.

The place was lit up like Fourth of July, creating a black as midnight expanse beyond its reach—where we waited.

We would have to go in hard and fast, Devil knocking out the cameras the second we made a move. Even if we put the exterior guards down quickly, it wouldn't be long before those inside knew something was up.

I expected they all wore ear pieces similar to ours, and a simple missed check-in over concern of the blown cameras would put the remaining guards on alert.

A handful of young women sat in a closed off, darkened room—perhaps the basement, but it was assurance Giada sat in an upstairs room with two other women, seemingly unharmed and healthy, had me itching to get to her *before* the guests arrived.

We had a half-hour if the information we'd been fed proved true.

It would take us that long to get close enough to infiltrate the place—if we were lucky.

Klingon's men would bottle up the front driveway on his command, keeping anyone who entered the estate from leaving once hell broke loose. The other road leading into the property was gated from a dirt road a few hundred yards to our south—and was our point of entry.

"Devil?" I spoke into my mic. "How's the south road looking?"

"All clear," his voice came through without a crackle of static.

"Let's go," I told the three men with me.

We made our way through the darkness. The night air felt balmy compared to what we'd left behind on the east coast, and sweat soaked my t-shirt. I swiped at my forehead, readjusting the goggles for a tighter fit and continued on sneaking through the desert landscape surrounding us, our footfalls near silent.

It took us a good twenty minutes to reach the road's edge, and I pulled my loaner gun from its holder at my shoulder. The three men with me did the same, attaching their silencers.

While Ryker would have preferred to use his knife to silence our first target, the guard stood inside the gate, safe from hand-to-hand combat.

Devil informed me that Giada and the two women with her were being moved downstairs to the main floor. Into a mirrored room—where a few men stood beyond in an attached parlor, out of sight, two deep in shadow.

Checking out the goddamn wares.

"How's the front looking?" Klingon asked through the earpiece.

A whispered "Third car entering the property now" reply came through seconds later.

We waited in silence for another fifteen minutes to make sure all the guests had arrived, and every second that passed seemed an hour—time enough for some fucker to get his hands on Giada.

"Devil?"

"All guests are in the parlor with their host. Two guards manning the parlor archway. Two at the front door. One in the security office. All three drivers waiting in the cars. Two on roof. Two out back. One by the basement entrance, one in the basement hallway."

I glanced at the three men with me.

Ryker gave me a clipped nod which the other two mirrored.

"Now, Devil," I said into my mic, having waited long enough.

"And... Done," he replied, but I'd already started stalking forward, gun up and aimed, knowing he'd knock the cameras out before I entered sight of one.

A silent pop dropped the gate guard and not one ounce of remorse hit me at the life I'd ended. I rushed forward as Klingon gave his men the order to block off the driveway with the two vans they sat in a block away.

The uphill sprint winded the men with me, but hours spent in the dojo and my attached gym kept me from fatigue. One guard on the veranda's side closest to us turned and walked back the way he'd come—none the wiser. They obviously hadn't gotten word the cameras had gone offline.

I headed for the basement garage door and entrance straight ahead of us, Ryker on my heels, as Klingon and his sniper slipped into the back gardens.

Another round from my gun put down the guard by the door, his cigarette falling to the pavement alongside his slack face.

Adrenaline rushed through my system as I stepped over the puddle of blood running beneath his head.

"Devil?" I whispered into my mic.

"I've got you on the feed coming straight through to me. Garage is empty. Guard still in hallway leading to the women."

I tried the door and found it unlocked. Ryker and

I slipped inside silently, moving quickly past the two black Chevy cargo vans parked inside—one bearing the license plate of Santiago. One less fucker to track down...

"Roof guards down," Klingon's sniper whispered in my ear.

"Veranda guards down," Klingon added seconds later.

"Driveway blocked—we're heading in," his VP stated.

Show time.

The interior door also turned beneath my gentle touch. One step in, gun at the ready, and the guard ahead of me turned—with a near silent *pop*, I put a bullet between his eyes before he could blink.

Santiago, I noted, taking a closer look while stepping past him. Fucker deserved worse for snatching my woman off the street, but I didn't have time to carve out his heart and slice off his balls.

We moved past the basement room housing the other women—the Vegas Vipers would care for them once we cleared the house.

I took the stairs two at a time, knowing I'd come out in the kitchen. While I could have taken the back hall into what led to the room where the three women were, I had personal business to attend to before retrieving my woman.

The man responsible for taking her was about to meet his maker—and I would be the one to send him to hell—after taking down every mother fucking guard and other sick bastard in my path.

24

GIADA

"Aline, step forward."

I recognized the voice of our gracious host coming through overhead speakers. My friend obeyed, her entire body shaking like a leaf, one hand covering her breasts, one the apex of her thighs.

"Remove your hands and turn in a circle."

She didn't move.

"Aline." His voice hinted at displeasure.

"Do it," I whispered fiercely at her.

Still, she didn't turn.

Buffalo Boy strode toward her, yanked her arms behind her back hard enough she gasped and arched, jutting her breasts out for the pervs on the other side of the one-way.

Silence descended, Aline's whimpers and Dianna's heavy breaths in my ears.

"Dianna, step forward," the voice said, and Buffalo Boy released his hold on Aline.

Dianna obeyed, her head down while doing as told. She dug her fingernails into her thighs, trickling blood over her pale skin.

"Turn."

She turned.

"Bend over."

A sob sounded—but Dianne bent halfway.

"Touch your toes."

Tears dripped onto the wooden floor as she bent, her bloodied fingertips touching her toes putting every inch between her thighs on display.

More silence from the mirror, and I fought to keep my chin lifted as my two companions cried.

"Giada, step forward," the sick squirrel stated as though bored.

I moved toward the one-way, stuck my tits out like a regal queen, looking down my nose at whoever leered at me through the dark glass, waiting for the command to bear my asshole and pussy to those wishing to own me.

The seconds ticked past. No one moved, no one spoke.

LYNN BURKE

I forced myself to breathe in to the count of eight and back out even though my insides quaked.

I am strong. I am badass....

No command came for me to turn or bend—a door opened to our left. Asshole host entered with three men on his heels.

The first gripped Dianna's arm and drug her kicking and screaming from the room.

I swallowed hard, but didn't move.

The second moved past me, a sneer on his face, licking his lips as he went for Aline. She went a bit more willingly, but her sobs ripped at my heart.

My fucking fault...

Asshole squirrel stood back by the doorway, motioning the man with his prize out past him.

I finally turned my focus fully on the third man studying me from his position to the asshole's right.

Black hair slicked back into a ponytail. Dark eyes, dead like a sharks, flitted down over me and back up, but without a trace of lust.

My stomach twisted, gurgling that damn alfredo I'd enjoyed as my new master—who else could he be—slowly smiled, a grotesque scar at the corner of his mouth twisting his lips into more of a sneer.

"Do you know who I am, princess?"

I glanced down over his Armani suit and the

232

shiny shoes on his feet. Manicured hands, I noted on my perusal back upward. Cleanly shaven like the asshole squirrel—but a good foot taller.

"I'm afraid not," I finally said, forcing myself to hold his scary as fuck gaze even though my insides quivered.

He chuckled, and I swallowed rising bile as he drew nearer to graze my cheek with the back of his knuckles.

My damn knees shook, and even though I lifted my chin in defiance, my body betrayed the fear digging its claws into my head.

He's going to rape me. Own me. Pass me around to his friends like a goddamn piece of cake for all to enjoy—

A shout sounded, and my owner jerked his head around toward the asshole.

I kneed him in the balls without thought, driving every ounce of energy I had into the thrust forward, grabbing his shoulders as he involuntarily caved inward—and I kneed again.

He shrieked like a little girl as the asshole jolted in my periphery.

A scream from outside the room sounded.

A shot.

Higher screams—then silence.

Buffalo Boy stood in the doorway facing outward, gun raised.

The asshole quivered behind the door.

I spun to dive out the door we'd entered through —and another shot sounded, pulling a scream from my lips as I jumped sideways.

Buffalo Boy fell backward like a freshly cut tree, lifeless, his chest a bloody mess.

Logan.

My breath left in a rush as he stepped into the doorway, gun at the ready in one hand, a bloody knife in the other, his pale eyes glacial as they flicked at me then to the man at my feet.

He scowled and took a step into the room, gun swinging to his right as though he knew without looking the asshole cowered there.

One muffled shot and the asshole slumped against the wall, a hole in his forehead.

A sob ripped from me, and I clasped my hands over my mouth, watching as Logan approached my would-be master.

"You." He spat on the man as though he knew him personally. "On your fucking feet!"

A bearded man I recognized from Cristian's grave side service appeared in the doorway, his glance quickly taking in the scene as the bright lights glinted off his sweat-covered shaved head. He, too, scowled at the man on the floor.

"Mother fucking cunt!" He rushed forward, pulling a big ass knife from his hip, but Logan put out his arm, stopping his friend.

"He's mine."

Dead Eyes pushed to a stand, still gasping and holding his balls—I hoped I'd crushed the fucking things.

"Stone. Ryker," he coughed out.

Both Vipers smiled, and shivers licked down my spine as they tucked their guns away.

I stepped back—giving them a wide berth since their eyes and their vicious looking blades promised death even though the man had greeted them by name.

"I'm sure we can come to an agreement." The man raised his hands, his dead eyes not so dead anymore.

My focus jerked between him and Logan who slowly moved forward, spinning the jagged-edged knife between his fingers. "Your days of dealing are over, Arturo."

Arturo...

A flicker of awareness shot through my brain.

Columbian cartel leader.

Father's campaign—the death threats.

"Oh God." I stumbled back another step, my focus on Logan who didn't spare me a glance.

He stood nose to nose with Arturo, his fisted knife arching to the side like he planned to throw a right hook.

"For Shaun," he whispered and slammed the blade buried deep in Arturo's side. Logan yanked it back out and flipped it to his left.

"For Warden," he stated a little louder, stabbing into his other side.

"And this, you sick son of a bitch—" Logan grasped Arturo's ponytail and yanked it backward, lifting his head "—is for even thinking about touching my woman."

A flash of the blade, and blood spurted from Arturo's neck as their gazes remained locked.

Gurgles sounded, and I stared in a fog, unable to think, unable to move, my ears beginning to ring.

Logan loosened his hold and Arturo crumpled at his feet. He turned toward me, the knife dripping blood at his side. His eyes cleared—and the pain, the longing, the fucking *need* slammed into my gut, keeping me from slumping over like a damn wimp.

I lurched toward him with a cry, stumbling in my haste.

He caught me against him with one arm, and I wrapped my body around his, needing to be closer.

The knife clattered to the floor, and I buried my face in his neck, the strength of his arms holding me tight, the scent of his sweat, his musk, flooding over me.

"I've got you, baby. Fuck, I've got you," Logan said, his voice breaking as sobs ripped from my chest.

Safe.

25

STONE

Someone threw a blanket around Giada, tucking it between our bodies to cover her nakedness as she clung to me like a leech.

I strode out into the parlor area and straight through to the arches as she sobbed against me, her hands grasping and her legs a vise around my waist. One arm under her ass, the other across her back, I continued right out the front door, bypassing Klingon and his Vipers who offered nods.

Volkov's guards and the would-be buyers sprawled all over the fucking place. The three drivers rested their heads against the driver seats, bullet holes between each set of eyes.

A van sat beyond, just inside the gate, the engine running.

Klingon's VP yanked open the side door for me as I approached, and I climbed into the far back seat, hidden by dark-tinted windows.

Settling onto the back seat, I shifted Giada away enough I could see her face in the dim interior light, the blanket sagging around her waist.

"Did he touch you?" I rasped, barely keeping hold of my emotions as kill mode adrenaline began to fade.

She shook her head, her eyes so damn green— like spring grass after a summer rain, tears clinging to her black lashes.

So goddamn gorgeous.

"I'm never letting you go, Giada. You belong to me—you understand?"

Another tear slid down her cheek as the interior lights began to fade and I tangled my hand in her hair and jerked her back against me, taking her mouth with bruising force, groaning as my dick swelled between us. Unable to be gentle, I soaked in her scent, her breath, trying to take her so far inside myself she'd never be free of me.

I had feared being distracted from what I needed to do when I finally moved into the only room the Vipers who'd stormed the front hadn't cleared. Even though Giada snagged my focus first, I didn't let her down. I'd turned to what needed to be taken care of without a thought—on instincts Pop's voice would never hinder ever again.

One bullet put down the fucker who'd thought to sell my woman.

My knife had brought the revenge desired by my brother and Shaun. It had been my pleasure to watch the life fade from Arturo's eyes mere inches from mine. My first kill with a knife—I'm sure I'd made Ryker proud, but once the threat had fallen, I'd been consumed with Giada.

The terror on her face, her wide eyes welling with tears... Ripped my heart to fucking shreds, but I knew she would be the one to put it back together—even if she hadn't agreed she belonged to me.

The salt of her tears laced our kiss, but she didn't pull away, didn't shy from my rough taking of her mouth.

"Need you," she whispered as I bit and kissed my way along her jaw, her hands shoving between us to grasp me.

Fuck, yes.

The adrenaline I'd been riding high on ebbed, yet a sense of urgency, of need beyond anything I'd felt before swept into its place. Uncaring of where we were, who stood outside the van's doors, I allowed her to free my dick.

I shuddered, holding her tight to my chest as she lowered her trembling body onto my hard length. She wasn't ready for me, but my stubborn girl worked herself downward with jerking shifts of her hips.

She whimpered when I finally bottomed out against her cervix, and I claimed her mouth once more, more than just *her* tears coating our lips.

It wasn't pretty—wasn't quiet or slow. The van moved beneath us, and when she shuddered, her pussy a tight satin glove milking me, I went off with a groan, every spurt of cum filling her, marking her.

Claiming her.

We didn't move, didn't speak for what seemed days, but in reality only long enough for Ryker and a handful of the Vegas Vipers climbed into the van. No one turned to look at us, and the driver simply pulled out of the driveway as I held my woman against me.

I didn't bother with a backward glance either.

———

Giada slept curled on her side, one hand beneath her cheek, her lips parted on soft exhales that moved the few strands of hair hanging over her face.

I gently tucked them back, but she didn't stir.

We'd arrived back at the Viper's club, shut away in the room Klingon had offered me and Ryker a few days earlier. I'd washed her in the small shower we shared, cleaning every trace of that goddamn time off her wilted body before ridding my own body of evidence of my ruthless killing spree.

She'd collapsed onto the bed, and I stayed beside her like she'd asked, ever vigilant even though the club promised safety.

Klingon had a cleaning crew assigned to take care of the mess we'd made. The bodies would be disposed of, the limos and cargo vans dismantled at his chop shop. The house itself would be sent up in flames—if it hadn't already been.

As for the other women—the two who'd been with Giada and the handful of others in the base-ment—Klingon offered to take care of that mess.

I had no personal interest in knowing his plans, so didn't ask. Giada, I expected, would want to know what happened to them, but until she asked, I decided to let it lie. Although I'd expected guilt or at least shame to hit me in the aftermath of the mess I'd made, no trace of either fucked with my head.

My cell buzzed in my pocket. They were ready for me.

Sure that she slept, I slipped out into the hallway and made my way to the back door to Klingon's office. His officers and Ryker already sat at the table, a laptop opened in front of the only empty chair.

"Have a seat," Klingon said.

I rounded the table—and found Warden and Vigil filling the laptop's screen.

"Klingon said you got her," Vigil said.

I sank into the chair and nodded.

"Arturo?" Warden asked.

"I made sure he knew who was sending him to the pit of hell," I said, my voice still scratchy from emotion.

"Tell us how it went down," Vigil said, "then you go back to your old lady while I talk to Klingon again."

I didn't lavish the story since I knew Ryker would once we got home. Sticking to the facts, I told him in my own words what I expected Klingon already had.

Vigil nodded when I finished. "Get some rest then get your asses home."

"Will do." I stood and strode back the way I'd

come in, hating I'd let Giada out of my sight for even ten minutes.

She stirred when I shut the bedroom door behind me, her lashes fluttering before she focused on my face.

I pulled my t-shirt off, slipped off my shoes and jeans, and climbed under the comforter.

"Logan," she whispered my name like a prayer as I wrapped her in my arms, her soft breasts against my chest, my leg between her thighs.

She peered at me, her eyes troubled. "I'm so sorry—I shouldn't have taken off like that. It was stupid. A rash decision."

"Shh." I smoothed back her hair.

"Please tell me no one was hurt rescuing me."

"A few scratches—nothing serious."

She hefted out a heavy sigh. "My selfishness is going to end in tragedy one day. I'm so damn disappointed in myself—"

"Stop." Acid burned my gut.

Her lips clamped shut, sleepy eyes blinking to wide at my harsh tone.

She hadn't responded when I told her she belonged to me while in the van, and the need to shield myself from hurt raged in my head—but her emotions, her thoughts were more important to me than my fragile ego.

I *loved* her, and she needed to know my thoughts toward her even if she didn't return them.

"Don't you every bully yourself—don't you ever repeat the bullshit your father fed you your whole life," I stated forcefully. "You have value. Worth beyond any woman I've ever met."

Tears welled in her eyes, but I wasn't done yet.

"You're fucking perfect in every way," I said, easing my tone and the furrow between my eyebrows. "Perfect for *me*, and I want you just the way you are, Giada Burtonelli. *You. Measure. Up.*"

She swallowed as a tear slid free.

"You're everything I've ever dreamed of, everything I could hope for in a woman. I'm never letting you go—and I mean that with my whole damn heart. I love you."

Laughter escaped on a sob, her smile wobbling as she touched a fingertip to my lower lip. "Say that again."

"I love you—so damn much I—"

Giada kissed me. Wiped every damn thought from my head with her softness, her sweet taste.

Groaning, I rolled her beneath me, and she wrapped her legs around my waist, but held my face in her hands, pushing my head back enough to peer into my eyes.

My dick jolted against the warmth of her pussy, and I moved my hips slightly, smearing my head in the slickness growing there. She still hadn't responded, but she wanted me, there was no fucking doubt about it—"

"I love you, too."

Well, fuck.

She dug her heels into my ass, pulling me closer, and I sank into her wet heat while holding her stare. Every damn wall, every shield crumbled between us, leaving us both raw and open.

"So much, Logan," she whispered. "So fucking much."

I took her mouth and showed her just how much I agreed.

26

GIADA

I didn't see Aline or Dianna again before leaving Vegas, but Klingon assured me they were being taken care of. Even though he was one big ass mother fucker, I trusted the sincerity in his eyes. He and his men had put their lives at stake coming for me—I doubted he would shed those women's blood to cover the Vipers' asses.

Sure, there had to be a mess to clean up at the house we'd been held captive in, but I had a mess of my own to take care of.

We arrived back in Boston, and even though Logan wanted to go straight to his house, I asked him to take me to my parents first. He wasn't happy —far from it—but agreed to sit in his truck while I went inside.

Having been buzzed in the front gate, Father's driver and head of security met me in the foyer.

"They're in his office," he told me, deadpan, but his eyes betrayed his unrest.

He'd seen and heard enough over the years to know what would go down. Nothing new under the sun on Father's part—but it was time for the final showdown.

One last bracing breath, and I opened the office door.

Mother hopped up from the couch beneath the window to my left, but Father barked at her to sit back down. She obeyed, the poor, poor woman.

"Where have you been?" he started as I moved toward his desk, but didn't wait for me to respond. "Do you have any idea the situation you put me in? Having to lie about your disappear—"

"Enough, already," I snipped, coming to a halt in front of his desk rather than hang back halfway across his office like always when getting reamed out.

He paused, and I took advantage of the silence.

"I've only come back to tell you I'm going to live my own life. I will no longer be bullied by you—your selfish wants and desires. This is *my* life, and you've no right to dictate how I behave and who I choose to allow inside my head and heart."

"You will come to heel like the little bitch you are, or so help me God—"

True laughter bubbled up and out of me, cutting him off.

He stared for a heartbeat as though registering what I'd just done. "There is nothing funny about this situation!" Spittle flew from his lips with every word.

"Your threats are meaningless, Nicolo," I told him, having already decided where he belonged in my life—*out* of it.

Mother gasped at my use of his first name, the first time I'd ever done so.

"You even try to touch me," I continued as he gaped, "and Logan will hand you your ass without hesitation."

"You think I'm afraid of a bunch of lawless bikers?" Nicolo straightened, righting his tie. "Loser gang members—I could take them down with a flick of my *finger*."

"I'd like to see you try." My chin lifted and my smirk remained after having seen what those boys were capable of. "If you value your life, don't cross the Vipers. They won't warn you with death threats —they'll just put you six feet under."

"Giada..."

I glanced at Mother. "Logan Stone is my rock, my home. He loves me unconditionally—as is. I've never felt that—"

"You choose him," Nicolo cut me off, "and you're dead to this family."

I met his penetrating glare head on, without faltering, the truth in my heart more freeing than any rebellious action I'd taken in the past just to piss him off.

"I'll choose him for the rest of my life. He's mine and I'm his. I'm one of the Vipers' family, now—and it's the best damn decision I've ever made."

I turned my back on the man who fathered me, a sense of freedom swelling inside me.

"You walk out that door, and you'll never step foot back inside this house!"

I paused to look once more at Mother. "You always chose him over us," I reminded her although it pained me to do so. "What has it gained you in this life?"

She stared, her lips parted—and I strode out without another word.

My heart slammed in my chest as my boots

clacked on the marble floor of the foyer. Stark silence lingered in the background.

For once, Nicolo Burtonelli had been left speechless.

Hysterical laughter burst from me as soon as I slammed Logan's truck door behind me, enclosing me in warmth from the cold day—and the chill my childhood home had seeped through my bones.

He drove out of the driveway while I had my off the wall meltdown. Once my laughter settled, he grabbed my hand and held it tight atop his hard thigh.

"You okay, baby?"

"Never been better." I beamed across the cab at him, and dark lust filled his eyes.

"Christ, your smile takes my breath away."

"Don't get any ideas," I told him, knowing right where his thoughts went to. "We've got one more stop."

He nodded, a soft smile pulling up his lips as he turned back toward the road. "I'm proud of you, Giada."

Simple words, ones I'd never heard from either parent, stole *my* breath. "I don't deserve you."

"The fuck you don't." His tone didn't allow for argument—so I kept my lips sealed and soaked in the love and acceptance he freely offered, the sense of belonging I'd been missing, the one thing I'd craved my entire life.

———

The entire left side of Marisa's face hid behind gauze, but one good eye met my gaze as I slipped into her room. Mother had texted me in Vegas that the doctors had stopped the sedation meds and she'd finally woken up.

"Hey," I said, moving closer.

The corner of her lips twitched. "Hey," she rasped a whisper.

I settled into the chair beside her and eyed the snowy-white bandages wrapped around her head. "How are you feeling?"

"Actually not that bad."

"That's the morphine talking."

Her lips twitched again. "Probably."

"So I wanted to stop by not just to see how you're doing, but to warn you about the shit storm you'll likely experience later today."

"Now what did you do?" Wariness filled her one good eye, but I didn't take it personally—no hint of anger or annoyance laced her tone.

"Basically told our father to fuck off."

"You didn't!" she breathed, her eye widening

"Yep. He threatened to disown me—and I walked out. All done." I wiped my hands on each other back and forth, as though washing them clean of Nicolo Burtonelli.

Marisa stared up at me. "Damn, I wish I had your balls."

I blinked, my hands falling to my lap. "What?"

"Do you have any idea how much I wish I had your backbone, Giada?"

Her words baffled me—I fucking stared, speechless. Miss goody-two-shoes, the obedient golden child was ... *jealous* of me?

"You've always stood up to him. Chose your own path. God." She shifted and winced, her eye shutting. "How I've envied you..."

I found my thoughts, my voice. "Are you serious right now?"

"More than anything," she whispered, peering up at me once more. "I always wanted to be like you —longed to have your spirit, your tenacity."

"And I've always wanted the love and acceptance you got from Father."

She huffed a snorted laugh. "Praise out the ass— but it isn't *love*, Giada. It's his own satisfaction over

LYNN BURKE

my conforming to his selfish wants to make him look good."

Holy shit.

Once more, Marisa rendered me speechless. Father didn't love her any more than me—his love didn't expand to those outside himself. Not even Mother.

Fucking *duh*.

"When you get out of here," I told her, "you make choices for you. Do what you want, you hear me? Choose the path you've always wanted. Forget about Peter Reynolds and find yourself some young stud who'll rock your world off its axis."

"Peter does do that for me," she whispered.

My mouth went guppy-mode. "Get. Out."

Marisa managed a shrug of sorts, her lips twitching again. "I love him."

"Well, holy fucking shit." I barked a laugh. "Okay, then. If he's it for you, who am I to judge?" My smile faded as thoughts of his relationship with our father flitted through my brain. "Does he treat you well?"

"He's no narcistic asshole if that's what you're asking."

"Does he *love* you?"

"Yes." Soft emotion filled her eye, welling it with wetness.

When I climbed into Logan's truck fifteen minutes later, I still laughed, and it was some time before I calmed enough to explain the one-eighty the relationship with my sister had taken.

Freedom from the Burtonelli name, freedom from the shroud draped over the connection I'd once had with my only living sibling.

Freedom to love.

Freedom to live.

27

STONE
ONE MONTH LATER...

Giada stood with Shaun and two other old ladies at the club's bar while my brothers and I discussed business. The lush ass wrapped up in tight as fuck jeans distracted me. It'd been over ten hours since I'd been balls deep inside my woman —too damn long. Those cheeks fit in my hands perfectly—my dick between them even better.

Giada was one *hell* of an addiction. My thirst for her refused to be slaked. The taste of her ... the scent of her, goddamn—

"Stone!"

I jerked my head toward Vigil across the table from me. His eyes glinted as the other Viper brothers at the table chuckled.

"Yeah?"

"Get your head outta your ass," Vigil said with a laugh.

"*Her* ass," Ryker corrected him with a grin— must be two sheets to the wind for him to smile like that.

"Fuck off, both of you," I grumbled and took a swig of my beer. "You're just jealous."

"Fucking right," Ryker slurred, pouring another shot into his glass from the half-full bottle of whiskey in front of him.

"So, as I was saying," Vigil said, drawing my attention from wandering toward Giada again, "Devil's picked up rumors there's a new Martínez cartel leader."

More than one curse rose from the men at the table.

"Don't know what you all are grumbling about," Ricky said with an annoyed huff while eyeing his double shot of whiskey fisted in his hand. "I told you if we took him out, the next in line would slide into place without a goddamn hitch."

"Thanks for that reminder, Mr. Know-it-all," Vigil ribbed his younger brother with a good punch to the shoulder, shifting him on his chair and sloshing his drink.

Ricky growled at him—literally—bearing teeth

and all while righting himself. Not the first time I'd seen the brothers act like a couple of rabid dogs.

"Any idea who?" Warden asked, sitting back and placing his hands on his thighs—probably readying to hop up should Vigil and Ricky decide to take things further, which they were known to do when a pissing match got instigated between the two.

"No names." Devil slouched onto the table, a sweating beer bottle in hand, when neither brother made a move to start a bare knuckles fight that would end up ensnaring half the club in a free for all just for shits and giggles. "Not yet, anyway."

"They're gonna retaliate, too," Ricky reminded us of the second thing he'd told us over a month ago.

"There's nothing brewing that I've seen," Devil said. "Not even a whisper of rumor it's the Vipers who did in Arturo and that Russian skin-selling prick buddy of his."

"Nothing?" Vigil asked, one eyebrow raised.

"Nope." Devil slugged down his beer.

"Klingon has more contacts than God," Ryker said, slamming down his empty shot glass and reaching for the bottle. "Coast to coast—he's got everyone in his back pocket. Squeaky clean smart mother fucker—always has been."

"Let's hope his cleaning crew did the job we paid him for," Vigil said with a grunt.

"So far, so good," Warden piped up.

I caught sight of Giada and Shaun sauntering toward us in my periphery, and I pushed back from the table, patting my lap, my mind and eyes fully distracted once more.

She set her fine ass on my thigh and draped her arms around my neck. "Hey."

I stared at her red-stained lips, plump as fucking cherries—delicious as the fruit, too. "Hey."

Her tongue flicked out over her lower lip, and I bit back my groan. Ten hours too fucking long.

"We left one hell of a mess," Ryker slurred, drawing my focus off Giada's face. "The bodies in Stone's wake..."

"Yeah, we've heard the story a million times," I said, shaking my head. Even though I didn't regret my actions, I didn't care to be reminded of how close to losing my mind I'd been—desperate as fuck to get my woman back.

"You should have fucking seen it," Ryker continued as though I hadn't spoken, lifting his glass and moving it sideways as though laying out the scene. "Running through those fuckers like a goddamn freight train. Ruthless. Fucking deadly." He slammed back his shot. "Just like your father's Bourne men, little girl," he said to Shaun. "It was a goddamn masterpiece. Boy made me proud."

"So you've said." She pursed her lips around a smile and shifted to straddle Warden's lap. "Thanks, by the way," she tossed over her shoulder at me.

"For?"

"The kidney stab in my name."

"My pleasure." I meant it, too. "Fucker deserved to die for all he's done to this club—and if the next head rises up against us, he'll go down, too."

"Hear, hear!" Ryker raised his glass, his face flushed and eyes glazed.

"Calm your britches, boys," Vigil said, killing the mood as others chimed in with agreement. "We're done with the cartel—staying the fuck outta their business."

"And when they *do* come knocking?" his brother asked.

Vigil's grin sent a shiver down my spine, so far from the good kind, my skin crawled. He'd been aptly named president of the Vicious Vipers— fucking brutal bastard.

"Heard Burtonelli is leading in the polls," Devil

changed the subject before fists flew, and Giada let out a groan.

"Different convo, please," my woman voiced with an eye roll.

"Where's his head at, Giada?" Vigil asked, ignoring her request.

"Don't know, don't fucking care. Haven't spoken to him or my mother since the day I left."

"Think that sister of yours could let us in on his plans for our fallout?"

Giada eyed Vigil with her backbone of steel, unmoved by his stare. "Probably," she finally said. "Nicolo doesn't know the two of us keep in touch. She's entombed at their house since getting discharged. If I asked, she might probe a bit."

Vigil nodded. "Ask. Tell her I'll make it worth her trouble."

An all-out dimple smile flashed across the table. "Dangerous thing owing that sister of mine a favor."

"Thought you said she's a meek little lamb?"

"She's grown some backbone of her own since being shot in the head."

"Good for her." Vigil slapped the table—his way of ending serious talk. "I need a whore to suck my dick!"

"God," Giada and Shaun both fake-gagged at the same time.

Vigil had no issue with their laughter and stood, adjusting his bulge right in front of Warden's and my old lady. "Someday a pretty little thing like you two will appreciate this cock as much as you do theirs." He cupped himself—and strode away in search of a wet mouth.

"Fucker," Ricky muttered, glaring after his brother.

Ryker just studied his untouched whiskey.

Warden whispered in Shaun's ear, and her face flushed. She hopped up off his lap quick as fuck. "See you all later!" she called with a smile, pulling Warden away as he stood.

"Time to head out?" I asked Giada, tugging on one of the long ringlets of dark hair hanging down over her breasts.

"Hell, yes."

"Lucky mother fuckers!" Ryker said as I stood, and I shook my head, not sure why the fuck he'd gotten drunk. The man could hold his whiskey—but not that night.

Devil muttered for him to shut the fuck up and Ricky finally slammed back his drink.

We strode outside, hands clasped tightly. Not

even April yet, and a warm front had pushed through New England. Giada hadn't even bothered with a coat over her long-sleeve t-shirt. I eyed the starry sky overhead and sliver of moon making its way across the expanse as we ambled toward my truck.

"Wanna go star gazing?" I asked Giada, pulling her tighter against my side and sliding my arm over her shoulders.

She grasped my fingers dangling over her other side. "If you're asking if I want your cock, that answer is always yes."

"Shit." My dick twitched at the sass in her tone, and I dropped my arm from her shoulders to grab her ass. "Where do you want it?"

"Anywhere—everywhere."

Christ, this woman.

"Fuck the stars. I want you home in my bed—our bed."

I pulled up beside the passenger door and pressed her back against it, holding her tight with my pelvis. She'd moved into my apartment above the dojo the day we'd gotten back from Vegas and sold her condo not long after. Every night, I'd made love to her, sometimes rough sometimes not—but perfect as fucking heaven every damn time.

Couldn't get enough.

"Our bed is my favorite place in the whole damn world." She smiled up at me, her fingernails scratching the back of my head.

"You mean that?" I asked, studying her face in the dim lights from the club's front.

"More than anything." Her eyes softened, the love and acceptance filling me full to overflowing like it always did when she looked at me like that.

"Then what do you say about making it yours—for *good*?"

Her lips pursed as she cocked her head to the side, faked annoyance unable to erase her smirk. "You're an asshole biker, Logan Stone. You're *supposed* to say 'you're mine', carry me off over your shoulder like a cave man, and don't give me any say in the matter."

"How about I just give you this instead and kiss you to seal the deal?" I fished the ring from my pocket I'd planned on using to propose after making love to her beneath the stars.

"Oh…" She lowered her left hand and I slid the ring into the place.

Her dimpled smile hit me in the sternum like a power punch, stealing my breath. "I'd have to say, *fuck yes* and then some, please."

I grasped the back of her neck and yanked her tighter against me, taking her mouth. She melted against my chest in complete submission, making me feel like I could conquer the world with her backing me for life.

Since rescuing Giada, Pop's voice hadn't once echoed in my ears. I'd found real love. Unconditional. And, I wasn't ever letting her go. If it meant being the alpha asshole she joked about, then I'd gladly be one.

I'd give Giada anything she asked—anything.

"You're mine," I told her, wrapping my hand in her hair and yanking her head back so I could see her swollen lips in the twilight. Pre-cum smeared inside my jeans at her gasp. "And you don't have any say in the matter," I growled against her ear and bit down where her neck met her shoulder.

She moaned, a shiver shifting her in my arms. "I want your cock inside me."

Fuck.

Who was I to argue? Screw making love under the stars. I swooped her up over my shoulder and stalked back toward the club.

"Logan!" she giggled. "What are you doing?"

"I'm cave-manning your ass back to the club for

one of the upstairs rooms." I swatted her ass, and she moaned.

Yeah. My woman owned me, and I couldn't find two fucks to give over anyone's thoughts on that matter.

THE END

———

ABOUT THE AUTHOR

Lynn Burke is a full-time mother, voracious gardener, and International Bestselling Author of hot romance books. A country bumpkin turned Bay Stater, she enjoys her chowdah and Dunkin Donuts when not trying to escape the reality of city life.

ALSO BY LYNN BURKE

Blood Born Series

Bonds of Worship Series

Darkest Desires Series

Dark Leopards MC

Devil's Outlaws MC

Elite Escort Series

Fallen Gliders MC

Found by Fate Series

Midnight Sun Series

Missing Link Series

Risso Family Series

Sandy Ridge Series

Vicious Vipers MC

Standalone Titles:

Abel's Obsession

Divulging Secrets

Healing Storms

In Between

The Playboy Bachelor